GLOBAL HERITAGE BOOKS
www.globalheritagebooks.com

William See, known to his friends as "Bill," is a physician and musician from Middle Tennessee. He is also known as "Tennessee Bill" and plays fiddle for The Glade City Rounders, an old-time string band. He is a horse enthusiast and a humorous storyteller. His southern voice is featured in the audio version of his books. He has previously published the fiction novel, *Sons of Barbee Collins;* the children's book, *Lulu Kissed A Caterpillar;* and *Index Bubble,* a work on economic phenomena and asset prices.

Special Thanks to:

Brandi Peetsch

Holly Horsfall

A Dozen

STRANGE

Tales

William See

Except for Chapter 10, this book is a work of fiction. Names, characters, places, and incidents are the products of the author's imagination. Any resemblance to actual events or persons, living or dead, is entirely coincidental.

The cover art features sections of John James Audubon's, *Great Horned Owl,* from Birds of North America.

Copyright 2022 Global Heritage Books
All rights reserved

First Edition Paperback

ISBN: 979-8-9858389-0-9

GLOBAL HERITAGE BOOKS
www.globalheritagebooks.com

Table of Contents

Frontmatter

Chapter 1: Man with a Past

Chapter 2: Brock the Buzzard

Chapter 3: Quarantine of Knux Patterson

Chapter 4: House on Fife Avenue

Chapter 5: Little Nicholas

Chapter 6: Beatrice

Chapter 7: Commedia Dell'arte

Chapter 8: Pocket

Chapter 9: Grey Buffalo

Chapter 10: Japanese Bullet

Chapter 11: Sensible Stranger

Chapter 12: Big Claude

Endmatter

Table of Contents

Chapter 1

Man with a Past

Pain was his first sensation. A throbbing head greeted his emerging consciousness as the current of the river pushed him partially onto its bank. He had been so close to death his mind had resigned to drowning, and his thoughts had ceased. His senses were merely a black canvas upon which nothing was projected. Yet, within his flesh, a spark remained. Though he no longer bobbed lifelessly in the drink, only his torso was pushed out of the water by the lapping surf. Without intention, his body took an agonal breath. This time his lungs were not deprived of the air they craved. Having not been denied, they took another breath. Refusing to die, his muscles twitched, though unguided by consciousness. A flickering impulse of life caused him to blink his eyes. For hours he continued to lay motionless as awareness evaded him. After a time, he blinked again. The blank canvas was disturbed, and a light appeared upon it. His soul stepped away from white light, not yet ready to give up its host. Again, he blinked. A wave of nausea prompted a heaving vomit of river water from his stomach and caused his head to worsen its pounding pain. He coughed as he faded in and out of awareness. He had no memory of what events preceded his confusing return to life.

He opened his eyes, but he could not endure their burning, and closed them tightly shut. He felt sand in his mouth and nose and water upon his legs. He opened his eyes again and fought through the burning pain to make out his surroundings. His mind formed thoughts. *Where am I? What am I doing here?* Then, more importantly, *Who am I?* His mind struck a blank. He racked his brains for any indication of a memory that might give him a clue to any of his many questions, but...nothing. Confusion and fear washed over him like the river thrashing over the rocks beside him. How could he not even remember his own name? He did not know the answer to any of these questions. His mind swirled as he made his first movements. He reasoned he needed to crawl out of the water, yet his legs would not move. He coughed water out of his lungs and tried again. With concentrated effort, his limbs began to twitch and move. Slowly, his actions became more effective, and he inched out of the water.

No shoes were on his feet, nor shirt on his back. Around his neck and shoulder was a satchel that contained only a soggy Bible. He moved his hands toward his face to remove some of the sand from his eyes. As his vision cleared, he beheld a long winding river, cut deep into mountains he did not recognize. He rolled his body to sit upright. Everything hurt. Examining himself, he beheld scars on his chest from heeled wounds unknown to him in addition to new gashes and scrapes.

The sun was high in the sky and warmed his wet face and head. He cleared more sand from his eyes and nose. Warily, he took to his feet, unsure of whether to trust his weak legs so soon. His legs obeyed, though his hips and knees hurt like they had been smashed against something hard. After moving up the bank far enough that his legs were out of the water, he moved toward a rock near the water on which he could sit. There were no trails or paths visible to him. The woods were dense all around him.

Again, questions plagued him. Who was he? Where was he? The only memory he felt sure he could rely on was that he was a Frenchman, yet his surroundings bore no similarities to his native country. If *this* was France, it was undoubtedly a remote corner, as he did not recall a forest this dense. Removing his gaze from his surroundings, he looked down at himself. He wore a pair of woolen trousers, torn badly at the right knee. He had no shirt, and assumed it was ripped off him during his time in the river. He sat bare-chested on the sunlit bank shaking sand from his hair. He examined his skin, searching for injuries. The only one that bothered him badly was on his head, and possibly explained why he had no memory. The right side of his forehead was contused and bleeding, and there was a wound that hurt to touch his fingertips to it. His head ached, even when he was not touching it.

As the sun moved slowly across the clear sky, he figured he had been sitting on his warm perch for about an hour. His trousers were dry, and the loose sand was now falling off his skin. With some help from a nearby branch, he made another attempt to stand. His steps were wobbly, but he managed to brave a few yards before sitting down on another rock. He ripped off the torn wool of his pants that flapped with his steps and began walking upstream along the river.

He was moving slowly north, but found the rocks of the bank difficult to navigate. The sharp granite cut his feet. He thought he would do better on the soft floor of the woods. Under the canopy, his feet welcomed the soft droppings of the conifers. This did not look like his home. He continued to search for memories. Who was he? He could not even recall a syllable of his name. His movements were slow through the woods, but there were fewer things to tear into the soles of his feet. He kept the glint of the river in sight as he made his way through the trailless woods. After stumbling around a few hours, he came to a soft patch of grass shaded by a great fir tree. He laid down gingerly on the green tufts. His head ached and was made worse by movement. He stared at the clouds through the boughs of the fir. Where was this place? What was his trade? He was no hunter. No fisherman. Definitely not a soldier. Did he have a family? How would he get home? Where was home? He thought, but nothing came. Which way should he go? He knew not. His confusion brought fear, and felt brief moments of panic.

The river's banks were narrow, and its obtusely angled rocks quickly became swallowed by the quaggy forest floor. Dense fir trees and hemlocks choked out the lesser shrubs attempting to grow beneath them. Among the firs and hemlocks were spruces and red cedar. Together they formed an endless field of stanchions supporting the dense canopy of green that allowed little light to pass.

He figured if he continued to travel upriver, it would widen, and he would see some man or vessel. He searched for any clue that would tell him what province this was. He was still dizzy, and thinking hurt, so against all of his instincts, he attempted to avoid it. He closed his eyes, hoping the darkness would aid his booming head. Lying still, his senses toyed with the long curtain of sleep. The vexation of his consciousness continued in his slumber and brought dreams vivid and irksome.

His first dream was set in the great dunes of a desert. It was a landscape of monotone hills. He knew it to be a faraway desert, though he had never seen such a place before. Through the hills of sand flowed a river in which he found himself swallowed in the water, then tossed upon the shore. He spat salty water and blood from his mouth. Then he beheld six banners belonging to six kings. He was instructed to pick the banner of his king, but he did not recognize any of them. "Then choose the banner of your mother's king," pleaded a voice, but he knew not the correct one. He cried out, "Who?" and awoke in a sweat among the tufts of grass. He again tried to form an image of his name upon his mind's tapestry but was not successful. He closed his eyes with hopes of prompting recollections. He hoped that he might calm his thoughts and memory would come to him. Though none came, he was able to drift into sleep once more.

A second dream took him to a round boat adrift on a river. Standing in the boat, he was knocked down by a violent collision with the bank. The boat began to spiral as it drifted down the river. A bearded figure approached him and said, "come, Raven!" then hurled him over the edge of the vessel into the water. The cold brine pulled him under, but he was able to claw his way to the bank. Using his arms, he pulled himself out of the water and onto dry sand. There he sees an olive tree. He knows he should pull up the small olive tree and take it to the master of the boat, but he is afraid to return. Instead, he builds a beautiful mansion, and the olive tree blooms into a great orchard. His eyes feast upon this beautiful place, and he wants to stay here forever, but is dragged away as wakefulness returned.

Night had fallen while he was in repose. He sat up and looked at the enormous firs and spruces around him as they towered regally in the darkness. The river in the distance reflected the moonglow in a million sparkles. He stood and admired the exceptional beauty. Walking through the spaces between the tree trunks, he followed the river upstream. His bare feet carried him until soft grasses again beckoned him to sleep.

A third dream visited him. In a deep wilderness, he hacked through a dense mesh of shrubs unknown to him. After many days of slow chopping, he found a group of men and their wives, also toiling through the vines. They, like him, knew not their names nor the country they were in. They caught great fish on which they filled their bellies and shared with all. However, they knew nothing of fire on which to cook them. He stepped among them and built a fire that astonished them. He then roasted their fish on a skewer over the fire. They feasted on the soft, flakey flesh. The strangers learned many things from him. They learned to make fire and become stronger and were able to cut their way through the jungle with greater ease. They came to love him for the things he was able to show them. They begged him to join their band and was going along with them, when again, he slipped out of the veil of dreams.

The first light of dawn appeared through the canopy. He stood and began taking steps through the cool woods. His legs hurt terribly, but he pushed through the pain with each step. Thirst was making its first request since crawling out of the river. Hunger likewise was plaguing him. As the sun rose, he could see the terrain of the woodland's floor as it sloped gently toward the river. Trudging on, he reached the edge of the flowing water, he kneeled and filled his hands. It was cold and clear. He drank another handful, then another, and could not recall a more refreshing drink. He sat upon a rock and was warmed by the sun. With his cupped hands, he lifted water to the seeping wound on his head. He washed and scraped dried blood from his face and neck. His hair was crusted together over a gash on his scalp. He began applying cool water to the matted hair and examined the separated skin under it with the tips of his fingers.

Overhead a great bird soared in the morning sun. It sailed from the trees behind him into an arch that led along the edge of the river just over the trees. At the other end of its pass, it curled into the massive trees on the other side of the river. After a moment's halt upon a limb, he returned to flight back down the river. This time its path was much lower and closer to the rock where the lost man was cleaning his hair. The bird was bigger than any hawk he recalled. Its black back feathers reflected a golden sheen. His head and nape of the neck were snowy white, as was its tail. He soared with ease, hanging his body under his wings upturned like that of a smirk. He descended toward the water, suspending his body just above the surface as if to land like a duck. While skimming within inches of the river, he grabbed at the surface. Then, with great effort, the bird lifted a fish from the water and climbed back into the air. The silvery fish, as long as a man's arm, fought in vain while suspended from the piercing talons. The great bird seemed little affected by the flailing of the fish. After a short flight, it settled upon the rocks next to the river. It stood atop the fish on a flat rock and tore into its silvery belly with its yellow beak. In a moment, the shining entrails were out. He continued to tear the flesh of the belly and enjoy the soft innards as well as a cluster of slick yellow eggs that spilled upon the rock.

The lost man watched the bird on its rock while resting his feet in the cool water of the river. He continued to pick the scabs in his matted hair. He plunged his head into the cold water, which stung the gashes and caused the bone underneath to ache. He pulled his head from under the water and sorted his shoulder-length hair, pulling it off of his face and looping it behind his ears. The bird took flight, having had enough. The fish left behind was devoid of entrails, but the meat of the body was barely disturbed. The lost man stood on his feet and headed slowly along the bank toward the remains. He pulled away some of the silvery scaleless skin and bit into the warm pink meat. He chewed, swallowed, and bit again, tearing away at strips, sucking it through his lips. The soft sweet fish was quite satisfying. What place was this? He recalled no such bird in France. He recalled no such fish either. This was not France. It worried him that he might be even more lost than he first reckoned. He stood and walked back up the sloping bank into the shade of the woods. He walked slowly with no destination in mind, only the hopes of a chance encounter.

He felt like he made three or four miles after eating the fish. That was enough for today. His head increased its pounding. When a sufficient glade of soft moss appeared amidst the woods, he sat. After being warmed in the sun before finding the cool moss, the shade welcomed him. He rolled onto his back, laying his head gingerly into the seafoam-colored moss.

He walked the next day, making slow, careful steps to avoid anything sharp and pokey under his toes. Moving slow was necessary in order to not rattle his head upon its perch, for it still pounded. The woods abounded with furry animals. Squirrels and chipmunks argued over rights to nut-bearing trees. He pondered if he could kill one to eat, for his stomach continued to growl. There were foxes with pups and friendly ring-tailed critters he had never seen. They fed themselves with their hands and stared like children through their bandit masks. This was not France. That night he slept some better, with the headaches slowly easing. He no longer saw red blood on his fingertips as he felt the wound on his scalp. That night his few dreams were brief and meaningless.

The morning was cool but bright. He wondered what odd sites this day would bring him. He returned to the river and washed the remaining dried blood away from the wounds that no longer oozed. Splashing the cold water on his face, he felt short whiskers on his face - a week's worth. He wondered where he was so recently where he might have shaved, but he did not know the answer. His empty stomach clamored for attention with increasing insistence. When would he eat again? At noon he observed the river to his left, widening and becoming shallower. Within a few hundred more paces through the woods, he saw it joined a larger flowing river. The forest in which he wandered was coming to a point in the fork of the two rivers. Once at the point of land, he discovered his small winding river to be an estuary of the larger one he beheld. Looking back down the other side of the pointed strip, he determined he was on an island formed on the side of the great water. Suddenly movement caught his attention. In the far distance downstream, something was on the water. A boat? Too far to tell for sure. It was going away, but it appeared to be driven by the occasional dip of a paddle by an occupant. It was too far away to shout, and the river was too noisy for it to be worth the irritation it would bring to his aching head.

Until now, there had been no signs of other men in this alien land. Neither did he know if his painful staggering had been observed by anyone. Indeed, he had been seen. Unknown to the lost man, a person had been watching him since his first steps along the bank of the river. His observer at first thought to kill the stumbling white man, but curiosity and a little fear held him in the shadows, watching.

To continue upstream, the lost man figured it was most practical to cross the river. There was a gray log caught and floating near the point of the island. He hatched a plan and decided he would ride it down the estuary and swim across the river with it. He pulled it loose from its jam, and soon he was neck-deep, crossing the small fork. His feet soon touched the smooth rock of the other bank. He continued his pace-by-pace trudge through the conifers, following the river, now on his left. This river was big - big enough for a galleon.

He applied more vigilance to scanning the water surface for another small boat with a paddler who might hear his cries for help. The same soft carpet of fir and spruce needles formed the forest floor on the other side of the river, but there were many more animals. Foxes, squirrels, masked ringtails, and now deer were never out of sight. No sign of a farm, carriage track, hoof print, or trail was found as he walked. It was beautiful. In the coming days, his headaches began to ease, enabling him to walk faster. If he only had shoes, he could cover five times as much in a day. He still had no destination, only the desire to find another speaking soul. His hope now was to find another person who might know the country and be able to provide food. As he walked, he carried a rock in his hand, hoping to strike one of the unafraid rabbits under the bushes he passed. He missed the first two but was successful on the third. The skin of the rabbit tore away easily, and he bit into the muscle as he had done with the fish.

He admired the beauty of the place. How expansive and wild. The weather was pleasant, and the trailless woods provided pleasant shade under the great conifers. His thirst was frequently satisfied by the clear streams he crossed that were feeding the great river. It had been three days since eating the rabbit, and he was looking for an opportunity to again address his hunger. He picked up another stone, which seemed ideal for casting at a rabbit or at one of the grouse or partridges that seemed to pay him no mind. His hunger pulled his attention from the wider river to the forest floor. He tumbled the stone around in his hand as he walked, familiarizing himself with its weight so his throw would be more accurate. He stayed on the ready as he walked; a few opportunities had been missed by not having the stone ready to fly. Ahead of him, a shape caught his attention. Between two firs, as if waiting for him to approach, was a man.

His silent watcher had grown braver having seen the clumsiness of the lost man, and the weakness of his steps, and so he stepped into view. His hair was long and black and pulled into a tangled wad atop his head. A band of furry leather around his head was adorned with a fan of jay feathers on the brow. He held a bow in one hand and three arrows in another, a string of fish was tied onto the back of his waist. He was small in stature but muscular, and hoped to take his new bare-chested and unshod prisoner without a fight. The stranger stood still and gave no appearance of fear as the barefooted wanderer approached.

The lost man raised his hand and waved. He smiled, but the stranger stood still, making no expressions. His bare feet began stepping again, "*Bonjour,*" he said, but the stranger stood steadily. "*Haloo,*" the lost man tried again. He continued toward the stranger until the gap between them closed. What was this place that holds such strange men as these? He continued to smile and extended his hand. The stranger looked at the hand extended to him and extended his hand to grasp it. The barefooted man did not know how to tell him he was lost but figured it was obvious. What gesture should he give? He placed a hand on his chest and extended the other, hoping to mime a plea for help.

The stranger wore thick leather moccasins and a cage of scraped reeds around his chest and arms. He gathered the arrows and bow into one hand, and with the other, pointed to the gash on the lost man's head. The lost man shrugged his shoulders, for he didn't know the answer. The stranger just stood. The lost man pointed at himself and then made the gesture of walking with his finger, then pointed at the stranger. This got no reply. "*Par les vous Francais*?" Nothing. He then pointed at the fish tied to the stranger's waist and gestured with his hand if he could have it. The stranger untwisted the strands and unstrung one of the fish, and handed it to the lost man. "*Merci! Merci!*" he said, bowing a "thanks" as his teeth tore into the meat. It was the same silver fish with pink flesh the bird dropped for him earlier.

A smile came to the stranger's face at the oddness of the man's hunger, and wondered why he didn't just go down to the river and get one himself. The stranger turned and began to walk away but turned and gestured for the lost man to follow him, which he did. The stranger was going slow to accommodate the barefooted man's slow progress. After a while, they came to a stream. The stranger squatted and filled his hands and lifted it to his mouth several times. The lost man followed suit while still studying his new rescuer. The stranger stood after he had had enough. With two fingers, he pointed at his chest," Nantahook." He then pointed the two fingers at the lost man and waited for a reply. The lost man opened his palms and shrugged. He didn't know the answer. The lost man pointed to the wound on his head to explain why he did not know his own name.

"*Je ne sais pas*," the lost man mumbled.

"Se Pa?" asked Nantahook, assuming it was a name. The lost man could only concur. Nantahook smiled and gestured to keep walking in the direction they had been going. Nantahook didn't say anything more as he walked, but occasionally looked back at Se Pa's progress. They walked until dark. A deep orange hue shined from inside the clouds as the sun began its descent in the evening. Nantahook pointed at a boulder that stood to their left between them and the river. Its size and shape were unique compared to the others they passed and was obviously familiar to Nantahook. When the duo reached the boulder, Nantahook pointed to the hollow in the rock, revealing the temporary abode it provided. He gave Se Pa another fish from the string while they walked down the river.

Nantahook was very patient and curious of the odd wanderer he found. He chose the easy paths for his new barefooted friend. Se Pa was likewise curious where this journey would end. Nantahook was obviously part of a larger village somewhere. Would the people be friendly? Would he be their next meal? As he slept with his belly full of fish, he hoped Nantahook's benevolence would continue. When the final fish of the string was consumed, Nantahook went down to the river. He produced a strand of vines, worn smooth and supple, from around the reeds of his chest ornament, and affixed to it a small hooked bone. It was sharp and adorned with blue feathers. He tossed it into the river, and with a few gentle pulls on the string coaxed a large fish to bite it. Nantahook pulled in the fish, added it to the string on his waist, and returned the hook to the water. In this way, he collected six fish from the river with ease.

With a few meals in his belly and his headaches slowly easing, he made better progress following Nantahook. Their second day together was spent walking and, as evening came, Se Pa wondered how long their journey would last. As dusk drew near, worn paths through the woods were visible. Se Pa's heart raced as he reasoned he would be in the village of others like Nantahook very soon. He also grew more curious of Nantahook's intentions.

As the trails widened, they were dotted with prints from smooth heelless shoes. The dense woods opened into a clearing of trodden ground. He saw a large structure. It was roughly fifty feet long and made of logs lashed together vertically. A layer of conifer boughs provided a roof out of which a fire smoked at each end. He saw naked children with long dark hair running in and out of the small square door on the front. When Nantahook walked past the building, the children stopped and stared at his trailing foundling with amazement. They had never seen a pale-skinned man like him.

Se Pa saw another, smaller plank and log structure behind the large one they had just passed. In the center of the village was a large gathering of stones. They were charred and ash-covered from years of use. The evening was laying its blanket of shadows over the village. Beyond the great fire stones were two rows of other lashed log buildings. Men with attire similar to Nantahook's were peeling logs, and bare-breasted women were working on their daily tasks, but stopped when Nantahook walked up with Se Pa.

Men began walking toward the two of them and spoke to Nantahook. Se Pa did not know what was being said, but could follow the hand gestures that indicated the river and him walking barefooted. The men's eyes were as wide as owls' while looking at the strange person brought into the village. Women came out of the woods to look at the odd pale man, but did not come as close as the many dogs and kids. The men and women had short, squatty legs but muscular torsos. The women were as wrinkled as the men, but twice as round. The smell of human filth was strong, as well as the stinging aroma of urine. This and the smell of rancid fish pervaded the air. Cakes of dung covered their arses, and all had decaying teeth. They marveled at Se Pa and walked slowly around him. They spoke questions to one another while Nantahook conferred with the older man with intensity and with many gestures.

It was dark now. Smoke was coming from the ends of the log structures of the village. Nantahook approached Se Pa and gestured for him to go into the round hole on the front of one of the log structures next to the great fire stones. It was barely big enough to fit through. Inside were women and children who were quite shocked by what had just stepped into the lodge. Nantahook, following behind, calmed them by making words to explain the finding of the pale man. Nantahook moved and sat next to one of the startled women. She handed him a joint of dried meat, upon which he chewed and gnawed. He spoke to the children in the pole building who were hesitant to come near the pale stranger. He then pointed to a soft pile of deerskin and rabbit furs. Se Pa took the invitation and sat. It was soft and comfortable, and he was grateful to have food and warmth. Nantahook took a joint of meat from one of the children and gave it to Se Pa. It was dried hard and was slimy with the child's spittle. Se Pa began to chew upon it and tear away strips of tough meat from the bone. A woman who appeared to be Nantahook's wife tore strips of brown meat from the long drying fish which were hung on the walls of the lodge. She then put them on one of the warm stones smoldering in the fire. The inhabitants of the lodge feasted on the warm fish and continued to chat among themselves about the strange occurrence. Se Pa wondered what strange sights this village would bring him in tomorrow's light. He laid back into the soft caress of the furs. He drifted into a restful sleep while the others around him stared at him in amazement.

The next morning, he was awakened by village children popping in and out of the round door of the lodge. They likely doubted the story they heard and had to see for themselves what the other children had rumored to them. Three of them were in the lodge looking at him when his eyes opened. When they saw him stir, they ran out screaming. Hearing men talking outside the door, he stood and walked out to them. There were seven of them standing near Nantahook. They stared at Se Pa speechlessly when he came into the daylight. These men were older than Nantahook and wore more elaborately decorated reeds and leathers. Children ran into the other pole houses to tell their comrades the pale man was awake. More men and women had come out of the lodges to see the spectacle. They used few words; they just watched him. To appear friendly, he strolled around the compound of buildings smiling and waving kindly to his curious audience. He could now see all of the structures of the village. Two small buildings stood in front of the two larger ones. A small building had been erected near the great fire stones. On either side were two trees that had been cropped and debarked. Around its gnarls and features were carved faces with large eyes and mouths. Some of the faces made very odd expressions and seemed humorous.

Se Pa was observing the faces carved into the tree trunk when an old and deformed person walked out of the building and into the middle of the crowd. He moaned when he walked, as if every movement hurt. His back was curved to one side, and his head came to a long flat point on top. He wore decorated bands of colorful feathers around the contours of his deformed cranium. The children and men came to him and helped him into the open. They revered him as if he were a holy man or shaman. He looked at Se Pa and then at Nantahook. Nantahook walked toward the old shaman and embraced him. They pointed at Se Pa as they spoke. After a moment, they finished speaking but stood watching Se Pa until the old shaman went back into his hut.

That night, a gathering was to take place. The shaman's hut would be filled to capacity by those eager to hear. Those who could not fit inside peaked through the gaps of the lodgepoles. The villagers were giddy as the day progressed, having more excitement than usual. As dusk approached, the oblong head of the shaman, who had been outside while the tribe was gathering, appeared at the door of his hut. He walked a few painful paces into the hut and sat down next to the warm fire stones. Nantahook and Se Pa sat next to him. Se Pa had no idea what was being said as the shaman spoke to the group in their native tongue, "Nantahook, we are gathered to discuss your new servant. Is your mind still the same?" asked the shaman.

"Yes," said Nantahook. The short, choppy words spoken in huffs meant nothing to Se Pa.

"Then you will go," said the shaman. The deformed old man then stood and removed himself from the hut, and several members of the tribe went with him. More logs were tossed onto the center fire. The air was warm and damp in the lodge, and bare shoulders glistened in the firelight. The odor was intense from the filth and fetid breath, and it turned his stomach. His ears were filled with the mumble of men and the laughs of children. After a time, the shaman came back in and raised his hands. The crowd quieted as he spoke to the group. "We see the pale man Nantahook has found. He is quite curious. He no doubt had fallen from one of the great boats that come to our river." Se Pa still had no idea what the shaman was saying but assumed he was trying to explain his appearance and possibly take credit for it.

As the shaman spoke, Se Pa heard the cry of a baby coming from a dark corner from behind the shaman. He was horrified to see two children lashed to planks, their backs perfectly straight. Tight bands of leather straps were around their heads and made tight by twisting them with thumb-length bone dowels. One of them was an infant, and the other would have been large enough to toddle. They whimpered in pain and pleaded for help. The plank and bindings around their buttocks were fouled with feces. One of the women moved some furs around the children to muffle their whimpering. Se Pa cringed at the torture these poor creatures were enduring. It was the same mutilation the old shaman had suffered that resulted in his deformities.

The shaman continued, "He is a friendly creature but will not serve us. He cannot hunt or even feed himself. His mind is like a dumb babe. He can't even smear dung on his shoulders to keep from burning in the sun. How does a man like this survive?" The crowd chuckled at Se Pa, the fool. "The gods will shine upon us if we lashed him to our lodgepole and opened his chest as we have done to those the gods have sent us before. We are a tribe loyal to the gods, and they have given us power over our enemies. Two winters ago, we saw Nantahook making sacrifices. He sent his firstborn to the rocks as we sang behind him. The gods have shone upon him and us. They have sent Nantahook this pale man, and he belongs to him. Nantahook? What will you do with him?" Murmurings swelled for a moment but dwindled when Nantahook made his statement.

"The gods have indeed been generous and have given us power. Last winter, when we went to the pale man's village, we were beaten away. They would not trade with us. For this, the gods have sent us a gift. The pale men who shape the stones which cut will speak to Se Pa. I will trade him to the pale men for the stones that cut." This brought more murmurs from the crowd. They still remembered when Nantahook and other men returned from their camp last winter, beaten up and empty-handed.

The shaman nodded and spoke, "The stones that cut will give our tribe even more power over our enemies. It is good." The meeting was over with these final words from the shaman. Some left the lodge, but most stayed inside to stare and tease Se Pa. General revelry continued into the night around the fire. Se Pa did not know what solution had just been decided but knew it pertained to him in the village. Nantahook was the man of the hour. Everyone came up to him throughout the night to discuss their thoughts with grim faces. As the night progressed, the numbers of those in the lodge dwindled, and the remaining conversants parted and went into their lodges. Nantahook gestured for Se Pa to come with him into his lodge. Like the night before, he was made to sleep on a pallet of furs near Nantahook. It was soft, and sleep was easy to find.

The next morning Se Pa was awakened by Nantahook's grip around his ankle. He was studying his feet and observing their size, much larger than any other man's in the tribe. Holding his leg up with one hand, he held up a piece of hard-dried deerskin against the sole of his foot with the other. He was to make Se Pa some moccasins. One of Nantahook's wives looked over his shoulder and took the dried deerskin after seeing where it should be stitched. With a bone awl and sinew fibers pulled from raw skins, she began forming the deer hide into a shoe. The soft deer hair inside would be a welcomed comfort to his feet.

She was a short woman with broad hips. The deep lines and wrinkles of her face conveyed a kind, but worried countenance. She squatted on the ground, working the edges of the skin with her strong fingers. She poked a series of stitch holes with the awl. With a piece of knapped flint, she snipped away pieces of the hide by wrapping it around a knot of wood and pressing into it with the sharp edges of the flint. She worked with intensity, but without hurry. Nantahook was only a few feet away, working to fashion straps onto a bundle of furs. He was much clumsier at the task than she.

He watched her fingers move around the stiff hide. She turned it around in her hands and looked at the row of holes she made with the awl. Not only did she want the shoes to be sturdy, but the spacing and aesthetic of the stitches also mattered to her. He was moved by her apparent empathy toward him and his painful bare feet. Her fingers tapped against the hairless side of the deerskin, and she proceeded with her handiwork. She worked silently. Her pointed bone awl scraped and poked into the hide like the long beak of a bird into sand. The sound caused tingles to shower from within his scalp, then move down his back, singing to his nerves like the gentle rasp of the cricket' as she gave his shoes her undivided attention. He thought of her existence here with the river people. Was it peaceful? Was she well treated? Se Pa was envious of the lifestyle of the tribe. He did not want to stay with them, but at this moment, he was very glad to have encountered them. They took pity on him, fed him, and clothed his feet against the rocks and brambles.

That evening the moccasins were finished. Their maker put them on Se Pa's feet, then took them off to make final adjustments. When they were to her liking, she handed them to Se Pa to put on. Then she stood up, twisted rabbit skin into the sides and top of the moccasins to make them fit snugly. Nantahook had also finished his bundle of furs' carrying straps. When Se Pa was walking around in his new moccasins, Nantahook walked over and placed the straps on his shoulders. They fit, and Se Pa was able to carry the bundle and walk through the woods. Nantahook nodded with approval. With two fingers, he pointed at himself, then pointed them at Se Pa with a walking gesture. Se Pa did not know where to, but he would be following Nantahook with his bundle of furs. A trading venture was reasonable to assume. Se Pa hoped whomever they may be trading with could tell him where he was. He continually searched his mind for any glowing ember of memory. Still nothing. No name could he remember. His mother? His father? His own? His kin? His profession? His skill? What was he good at? Nothing came to him.

Their journey began the next day. Without much warning, Nantahook walked over to Se Pa and smiled. He squeezed the muscle of Se Pa's right arm and gestured "walking" with his two fingers. He pointed at the bundle of furs and intended for Se Pa to don the pack and follow him. With the pack on his shoulders and his new moccasins on his feet, they began walking south.

The path they followed was wide and smooth from footsteps. It wound through the trees and water-worn boulders. The path was made from thousands of feet over thousands of years. Feeling better and having decent moccasins allowed him to walk at a man's pace. He kept up with Nantahook, who was not moving exceptionally fast, but steady. They both looked for berries and shrub roots to eat as they walked. Before the end of the first day's walk, Nantahook took his hook and string to the ever-visible water's edge to retrieve four fish with ease.

That evening they built a small fire. From a pouch tied to his waist, Nantahook produced a small chunk of wood that fit into his palm. In the center of the piece of wood was a charred divot. As he had done many times before, he started a fire by spinning a dry twig into the oily divot. Holding the piece of wood between his knees, he knelt upon the ground. After breaking a dry twig from a dead fir tree, he ground one end against the rock until it formed a dull point roughly the shape of the divot. Within a few minutes of spinning the twig in his hand, the small chunk of wood began to smoke. He placed a few pieces of dried plant fibers in the smoking divot as he continued to spin the twig. After a few more minutes, tiny orange flashes of flame appeared, which he kindled with more plant fibers and puffs of air from his lips. Se Pa mused how much easier the task would be if Nantahook had fish oil or cotton wicking, but Se Pa had no way to tell him. As a small flame grew, he added more plant fibers and kindling. He nursed this into a licking fire. With other sticks, he impaled the fish and propped them over the flame. The smell was delicious as the pink fatty meat sizzled. Sleep was easy that night with full bellies.

The next day's walk was much the same. Early in the day, they passed three men along the trail. They were dressed much the same as Nantahook, but the nature of their journey was not obvious. They carried nothing other than wooden spears for fishing or gigging small animals. Later that evening, they passed a series of large houses similar in design to those of Nantahook's village. Nantahook guided Se Pa around the village, even though a path went through it. It was obvious he did not want to enter without an invitation or a gift. It was night when they passed the village. Nantahook did not build a fire, but instead, peeled pieces of raw fish from the two still tied to his waist. Well into the night and far enough from the village to not offend, they found repose under a large conifer with the soft mound of needles beneath it.

They would pass other villages with large lodges houses made of logs in the days to come. Nantahook navigated around them each time to avoid any confrontations. The journey would take two weeks, yet Se Pa never knew how far they were into it. After a week of walking, the river, always on the right, grew wider. It had grown steadily so during their journey, but now it looked like a sea. Waves rolled against the bank and tasted salty. The river had emptied into the ocean, and now they found themselves walking along an oceanside path that grew wider and more worn. Passersby were more frequent. Their feathers and attire were also different, yet they were still able to communicate with Nantahook. After three days along the sandy trail, the path revealed unique marks. They were oxen tracks and wheel marks. Who made those? Were these white men? The tracks were made by wide roughhewn wheels, and he hoped their makers could tell him where he was. Could there be a Frenchman among them? Were these the people Nantahook was taking him to? Was Nantahook trying to help him? For two more days, they continued down the path, following the oxcart tracks.

The path widened and often resembled wagon roads. The trees also grew in enormity. Se Pa had never dreamed of trees so big; so big ten men could not reach around it. The trunks bore deep valleys and gouges. Se Pa's vision was not poor but was not good enough to see the tops of these behemoths. They passed more men and occasionally women on foot. They wore garments much different from Nantahook's and featured much finer stitching. They did not seem surprised at the sight of Se Pa's pale skin and growing beard. Had they seen others like him? Two more days of walking would reveal the answer.

The woods were dense and beautiful. The trail now was muddy from its frequent use. Oxcart tracks were abundant, but he saw not a single round hoofprint of a horse. Alongside the trail, Se Pa noticed a tree. Chop marks from an ax! Men accustomed to the same iron tools as him had struck this tree. He felt a tinge of excitement. Soon after, he saw a field that had been cleared and planted with crops. This intrigued Nantahook as the methods were foreign to him. There was smoke rising from the trees ahead, and Se Pa thought he smelled coal smoke. Nantahook seemed more apprehensive about his surroundings and, after a time, gestured for Se Pa to walk ahead of him.

As they continued, the pair saw a row of log fortifications, but unfortunately, seemed of little use due to their disrepair. Behind them were log houses with stone chimneys. Se Pa was anxious to approach one, and he picked up his pace with optimism. He soon stepped into a paddock between two large log houses. "*Bonjour! Haloo?*" shouted Se Pa. No answer. "*Bonjour!*" Soon a dark-skinned woman in a mixture of wool and skin clothes stepped out and looked at him. She went back inside the house, and a moment later, a man stepped out.

He was about Se Pa's age with a full dark beard. He wore skin clothes but was a white man. "*Bonjour, Monsieur.*"

"*No dice Francais*," said the man and pointed to a smaller log structure. Further down the path.

"*Merci*," said Se Pa. He and Nantahook walked toward the log cabin at which the man pointed. Behind this cabin was another man. He was scraping hides. His clothes were also leather, but his hair was gray and tied behind his head. "*Bonjour, Monsieur,*" said Se Pa. The man stopped and turned around. It had been quite some time since he had heard the words of a fellow Frenchman.

"*Bonjour,*" said the man. "Where did you come from?" He asked in French, sweet to Se Pa's ears.

"Friend, I do not know. I was injured and lost. I cannot recall my name nor the name of my home. I cannot tell you the year. And, I know not what place this is, other than it is not France."

"Indeed, this is not France." The man stood still and pondered the idea for a moment. He wondered if such a circumstance was even possible. "How long ago did you arrive?"

"*Je ne sais pas.*" He continued to explain in French. "In fact, my finder here, Nantahook, calls me 'Se Pa' due to my unsuccessful attempts to explain myself."

"Well, this is an odd bird," said the Frenchman.

"What is your name, friend?"

"Manière," he said.

"What place is this?" asked Se Pa. Manière laughed.

"The Viceroyalty of New Spain."

"New Spain?"

"Aye," said Manière. "I'd say you were on a galley, lost a sea." Se Pa began to ponder the possibilities of how he could have been carried so far from France. All the way to the New World. "You remember nothing?"

"No," he spoke. He wished for a skill to announce that would perhaps be useful to the group. "Nothing." He had scars on his back. Both new and old, but he knew not what skirmish made them.

"Perhaps a priest?" asked Manière in jest, suspecting him more likely a bandit. Se Pa had considered it. He could recall a few prayers in Latin but assumed he learned them as a child, yet he could not recall the name of a single childhood familiar.

Se Pa nodded. "Aye, a priest or a ship's mate, though I recall no skills of either. I sincerely do not know, *Monsieur*." Manière studied Se Pa. He looked at Nantahook, who was still behind him. He spoke a few coarse words to Nantahook in broken Chinookan[1]. "You have returned? You bring white man?"

Nantahook nodded, and replied in the native language. "I found him stumbling along the river. 'Se Pa.' I trade him to you for the rock that cuts."

Manière laughed and turned back to Se Pa. "Your friend says he found you and wants to trade you for an ax. Are you aware you were entered into this arrangement?" Se Pa smiled at this ignorant irony. Nantahook saved his life. He gave him food out of kindness and brought him here. Nantahook was his rescuer. If Se Pa owned an ax, he would have given it to Nantahook with thanks, but he had nothing. He realized how desperately Nantahook must have wanted an ax that he would be willing to come this far to risk another roughing-up from the annoyed white villagers who did not have enough axes for themselves.

---

[1] The language of the Chinooks, A native tribe of Northwestern North America.

"Do you have an ax for which I could indenture?" asked Se Pa.

"I guess you are a priest. A French first mate would have already run this poor fellow through," said Manière. "No, there is no ax to trade. Besides, one preacher with no skills is no trade for an ax. There would have to be five or six of you, blonde, of course, and lay eggs too."

"Do you have an old iron blade?" asked Se Pa. Manière sensed the genuine request and Se Pa's genuine appreciation of Nantahook. "If you had such a thing. I would happily assist you in your work here until such time I pay off the debt." Manière grumbled and walked over to the fireplace and removed a blank rod of metal that had been beaten flat at one end and sharpened. It was a rough piece, but it would suffice. The flattened blade was as wide as a man's finger and about as long. The thin iron rod at the end was about six inches in length. Manière handed it to Nantahook.

"Don't have an ax!" Manière said to Nantahook in Chinookan. It was not an ax, but this iron blade would have many uses and made the risky trip worthwhile. Nantahook dropped the bundle of furs from his back and looked at the blade. He eyed Manière and Se Pa, then nodded. He took two steps backward before turning and walking out of camp. Se Pa never saw him again.

Manière was tall and solidly built. He was a fearsome sight to the natives, being so tall and broad-shouldered. His hair and beard were white. He tamed his hair with goose fat and trimmed his mustache into a Dutch vee. He carried a regal demeanor and enjoyed a vulgar sense of humor. Se Pa never asked him about the native woman that stayed with him but assumed he traded an ax head or some such thing for her. He scolded her often, but generally cared for her, and she cared for him, though he did not call her "wife." Manière called her "Feather," not bothering to learn her given name. In the coming months, Manière and Se Pa would have much to talk about. Manière was the only Frenchman around and appreciated being able to banter in his most apt tongue. It was a welcomed change from the stiff Spaniards in the compound. Both men were curious, if not suspicious, of the other and indeed wondered what nefarious acts had gotten the other where he was. Se Pa did not know his own circumstances, and Manière did not care to reveal his. They enjoyed their nightly chats by the dying fire before sleep.

"So, you recall nothing?" asked Manière.

"Nothing of use," replied Se Pa. Per usual, Manière merely stared into the eyes of Se Pa, looking for a glint of a lie. Se Pa had nothing to hide from the piercing eyes above the twitching mustache. "What is the name of our king?"

"Dear God! You mean nothing!" Manière laughed. "Louis XVIII[2] a real saint."

"Of Spain?" asked Se Pa.

---

[2] Louis XVIII was king of France until 1824 when he died and Charles X was given the crown.

"I heard as of last year it was still Ferdinand.[3]"

"There are Spanish galleons that come into the river?" asked Se Pa.

"Aye, lost ones, but I've not seen one of them in a while." After silence, Manière asked, "Was it a blow that took your memories?"

"Yes." Se Pa pulled back his hair to show the still healing gash and dented skull. Releasing his hair, he asked, "Manière, what brings a Frenchman to the Spanish New World?" It was a question Manière could not escape.

"I was a sergeant in a regiment aboard *Le Mouette*. A Spanish gunner sunk us, and I was taken prisoner to Manilla. We signed on a treaty, and I was to be unbonded if I signed on as mate for the years. I agreed, but after a while, an 'opportunity' arose to detach myself from indenture." Manière showed he did not intend to answer any more questions of this type by the expression on his face. Se Pa changed the subject after a moment of silence to show he understood.

In the coming days, Se Pa found Manière to be gruff and quiet but still pleasant company. There was never any overt talk of indenture because it was not necessary. Se Pa had nowhere to go and now depended on Manière for his survival after departing from Nantahook. The first night Manière made Se Pa a pallet of furs in front of the fire. The dark-haired

---

[3] Meaning: Ferdinand VII King of Spain until 1821.

woman made a rabbit stew while the two of them sat exchanging occasional questions but mostly wondered silently about the other's circumstances.

Se Pa recounted more details about finding himself in the river. Manière felt there was significance in the satchel and the Latin Bible. "You carry the demeanor of a priest," said Manière, "Do you feel the calling within you?"

"Not exactly," replied Se Pa. "I certainly do not feel holy, but I guess it is possible."

"Se Pa is not a fitting name for a Frenchman. Perhaps we should call you Saint Paul." Meniere smirked, thinking himself clever. Se Pa smiled back at the probable irony, but the name stuck.

The rabbit stew was making Saint Paul sleepy. He snuggled into the soft furs. "How many traps do you have?"

Manière thought for a moment, "a couple hundred, I guess."

"When will we check them?" Saint Paul intentionally used the word "we" to ensure Manière knew his hospitality was appreciated.

"Tomorrow."

"Aye," said Saint Paul with every intention of being a helpful companion.

He found the days spent checking traps pleasant. It was often strenuous and occasionally cold when the weather was inclement, but the wilderness was beautiful. It abounded with all sorts of creatures he had not seen before. There were moose, deer, exotic geese, and exotic natives. The work was hard, but Saint Paul liked it. They were primarily looking for otters and beavers, which were becoming increasingly scarce. However, their bundle of hides increased in size daily. Saint Paul prepared for the eventuality of taking the hides north when Manière would sell them to the ships that dock in Shoalwater Bay.[4]

Manière knew very little about anything outside of the territory south of the big river with many names. Nantahook had called it "*Wimal*," but Manière usually referred to it as "The Big River."[5] The generous Frenchman was an expert when it came to navigating the marshes and the soft coniferous forests. He was a proficient trapper and traversed his range with otter traps he made himself, placing them in the streams when spaces between the banks were ideal. Despite this ability, he was usually unable to answer Saint Paul's questions about France or Spain. Manière spent some time on a French merchant vessel as a young man before being taken prisoner by a Spanish warship. Manière only grunted and was not interested in providing any details when Saint Paul asked about his escape. Being a trapper south of "The Big River" was a good place for anyone to hide. The men he traded with were all Spaniards, but he seemed to have no fear of them.

They worked all winter collecting hides from Manière's traps. Other men and their wives who had cabins

---

[4] Today is known as Willapa Bay.
[5] Today is known as the Columbia River.

nearby would all make the journey with their hides to Shoalwater Bay together. Saint Paul was not quite sure what would become of him after the day of trade. Would he get on a ship? If so, where would he go? To Spain? If he did make it to France, where would he go? What skills did he have? Of what use could he be?

The snow was deep and piled in deep drifts in many places. When it was falling too fast to check the traps, they stayed in Manière's warm cabin. Saint Paul contemplated the life of a trapper and wondered if that was his most practical future. Would he partner with Manière? He had not discussed it with him. He was curious who and what type of men he would meet there. Saint Paul found himself in silent mediation in the corner of Manière's cabin. The crackling fire and whistle of the winter wind filled his ears, and he imagined his possible past. He had little anxiety about his future, for he knew so little of the world outside his wild corner of New Spain. On days when the snow let up enough to see, Saint Paul and Manière donned snowshoes, checked traps, and added to their growing pile of furs.

The winter raged and passed, and the sunnier days of spring began. The sun shining on the wooden planks melted the snow, and metronomic drips of water fell into puddles along the outer wall. Other trappers in the cabins nearby also had large piles of furs ready to sell. The lot of them would eventually travel north as a cohort with loaded oxcarts and packs of furs on their own backs to the mouth of the Big River.

Saint Paul was resigned to any eventuality that presented itself during this journey. If the group of trappers was open to him staying with them, he would accept it. If it seemed appropriate to board a ship tied in the river, he would.

The day had come. The carts were loaded with bundled furs, and the men and their wives headed north. They traveled a week before reaching the mouth of the big river, and when they arrived, they planned for three of their men to cross and make their way to the ships tied close to the bay. There they would make arrangements for a boat to come to the southern bank of the mouth of the river on which they would load the furs. Once on the southern bank, the men conversed and decided who would go. Saint Paul volunteered. Two other men, Spaniards, would join him. The others would make a camp and tend to the bounty of furs while the trio arranged for a boat.

The next morning Saint Paul and the other two men, Alvaro and Mateo, set out with bundles of furs on their backs down the bank in hopes of finding a native with a canoe to take them across. Alvaro had been in the country his whole twenty-seven years of life and spoke Chinookan well. After a half-day of scanning the water, Alvaro began waving at two men in a canoe. The paddlers had long dark braids and red bands and reed cages around their arms, similar to the ones Nantahook wore. The canoers paddled toward the group, and Alvaro began to speak to them. He offered them some of the furs from their bundles if they would paddle them across the river, an offer they accepted. They had muscular torsos and were quite adept at maneuvering the canoe in the current. Once on the other side, the furs were paid, and the trio continued north.

After two days of walking toward the sea with the Big River on their left, an indent in the contour of the bank created a smooth area of the river where three ships with sail-less mast poles were anchored. Mateo called it Baker Bay. As the three of them approached, they could see rough log structures with white men milling around them. There were smoking fires and stacks of furs soon to be loaded onto the boats. There were also a few dark-haired natives, but they kept a distance from the Spaniards. Some of the buildings were surrounded by log fortifications and did not look old. The ground around the buildings was muddy, and the smell of cooking meats was mingled in the smoke. Mateo spoke a few Spanish words to some of the trappers they passed. Around one of the buildings, the trio spotted uniformed men, which Saint Paul assumed were captains and mates of the anchored ships. Mateo moved toward them and began to speak. He was directed toward a gray-haired man with a twisted mustache and a red wool cap. Mateo began a conversation with him while Saint Paul strolled around the buildings.

Mateo returned to the trio to inform them one of the boats would be setting sail in a week and would make a stop on the other side of the river to purchase their furs. They had accomplished their task. They decided to camp within the fort that night and begin their trek back across the river to their comrades the next day.

As dusk settled upon the fort, the stark white half-moon was reflected in the millions of small ripples in the bay's water. The seemingly infinite forest near this part of the river was dense with hemlocks. Among them were huge and ancient red cedars. The screeching gulls and cormorants argued back and forth. A fire had been well stoked, and several trappers had gathered round to converse and grumble. Saint Paul regarded their deeply lined faces as those of unrelenting tenacity. The wary natives were near and almost silent but did not share the fire with them. The men talked of frequent strife with the Chinooks and other tribes in the area. Most of the men spoke of them as ignorant savages who stayed drunk and would trade their children for iron wares. He recalled Nantahook, who had shown him kindness.

Some of the uniformed men from the anchored ships were finished with the day's counting and business, and were eager for conversation. They strolled toward the fire and sat upon logs to join the trappers. They spoke in Spanish. Saint Paul did not understand many of their words, but he could tell from their gestures of frustration and disgust they were speaking of quarrels and battles. Alvaro and Mateo questioned the captains and mates regarding these contests for power.

One of the men among the captains was older than the rest. His face was brown and weathered. He wore no uniform, but instead donned a burgundy vest over a stained white shirt and olive trousers. He accompanied the uniformed Spaniards and must have seen a thousand voyages. He sat quietly and unsurprised by the stories of war combat at sea and clashes with natives, as if he knew these things were part of an inevitable and unending cycle. The old gray-haired man, who the captains called "Ferd," stared curiously at Saint Paul. He looked at him with eyes that seemed to recognize him. Saint Paul noticed he was being studied and nodded cordially to Ferd, who nodded back. Through the night, Ferd said nothing but his visual study of Saint Paul was unceasing. He tried to say a few words to Ferd, who only expressed ignorance of the French words. Eventually, the men became sleepy and tired of conversation, and one by one, found a place to sleep. Saint Paul was among the last to leave the fire, as was Ferd, who nodded a silent goodbye when he joined the Captains to sleep in the decorated cabins aboard the ship.

The next morning, Alvaro and Mateo were up and ready to go. Saint Paul noticed the captains and mates were back conversing with one another near the fire, and Ferd seemed to be giving advice to them as a group. Saint Paul detected frequent looks in his direction and perceived they might be talking about him, yet he assumed Alvaro and Mateo had told them of his story, and how he had no memory of anything before being found by a native. He smiled politely back at them. Shortly, two of the captains began to walk slowly toward him. Ferd came behind them. "*Senior*," one of them said. May we speak to you?" asked one of the captains.

Saint Paul smiled and replied, "*Parlez-vous France?*"

"Yes, *Monsieur,*" spoke the Captain in French.

"Yes, of course, it would be my pleasure." Saint Paul looked forward to the Captain's curiosity, hoping to collect some clues about his past.

"My name is Captain Barros, and my colleague here is Captain Lorenzo."

"It is a pleasure to meet you."

"What is your name *Monsieur?*"

"Alas, perhaps you have heard of my fate? My recent acquaintances call me Saint Paul. However, I do not know my Christian name."

"How can that be?" asked Captain Barros.

"It was last summer when I found myself nearly dead and drowned on this very river. I cannot tell you how I came to be in this country. I cannot tell you how I came to be displaced in this river. A native found me and brought me to the trappers. Is it possible that I know you? Or *you* know me? I am searching to know what possible past I may have had."

"Very interesting. I am sorry for your misfortune," said Captain Barros, "I, nor Captain Lorenzo, have had the pleasure of meeting you previously. It is our old shipman, Ferdinand, who thinks he might have." Saint Paul gasped with excitement. It *was* a look of familiarity that old Ferd had cast at him around the fire last night.

"How grand!" Saint Paul had conjectured many times that he must have had an extensive life at sea to be a

Frenchman so far from home. "In what capacity may I ask? It is wonderful that fate has brought you to me that I might know something of my past."

"That part is also interesting, *Monsieur*. In fact, he says you are notorious." The Captain squirmed awkwardly as he searched for the words to say. "He knows you to be the man who slit the throat of his captain and made away with that ship's gold." Captain Barros stared into the eyes of Saint Paul after saying this. Saint Paul turned pale. The elation of having met a potential familiar instantly vanished. He could say nothing. Surely it was not true.

"No, that simply cannot be! I assure you I have no sentiments of violence. He must be mistaken. It must have been some other occasion from which he knows me, if he knows me at all."

"I understand your shock, *Monsieur*, if what you say about your recollections is true. However, Ferd is quite certain. We have found this old seadog to be quite correct about most things as long as we have known him. He has seen much of the world, including posters with your likeness."

"No, it just simply cannot be. He must be mistaken." He noticed Captain Barros' countenance slowly firming. Captain Lorenzo and Ferd moved slowly behind him as if to apprehend him if he attempted to escape. Saint Paul made no attempt and simply repeated, "it cannot be." Captain Lorenzo and Ferd came closer to him, each grabbing an arm. Saint Paul still made no efforts to escape. Ferd produced a short piece of rope and began to bind his hands.

"*Monsieur*, we firmly believe you are Gaston Tremaine, most recently was known as 'Padre Gaston.' You have no belongings whatsoever? Nothing to prove who you are or are not?"

"No *Capitan*, nothing. When I crawled out of the river, I was nearly naked and had only a satchel and a Bible." After saying these words, the water-logged Bible made more sense. Could he have been masquerading as Padre Gaston?

"I am willing to believe you do not remember, you seem genteel enough, but again you are known for winning confidences. Monsieur Gaston, you are indeed guilty of many crimes. Your absent recollections do not exonerate you from the murders you have committed." Gaston was silent and wholly in shock. "Furthermore, *Monsieur*, over the winter, we heard you were discovered aboard the *Isabella* and were keelhauled[6]. The story that was passed among the sailors was that, in your typical fashion, you were posing as a priest and asked for passage, then your plan of murder was uncovered. You were hauled under but found alive and taken under again. While pulling up the second time, you became unbound. They searched but never found your body." Captain Lorenzo

---

[6] Keelhauling: A punishment administered at sea in which a person was bound with two lines looping under the ship and dragged from one side to the other. Frequently deadly and always disfiguring due to severe lacerations caused by sharp barnacles growing on the keel of the ship.

and Ferd pulled up his shirt to reveal the healing gashes and confirmed their suspicions.

He was taken and bound to a pole inside the fort. There he sat in quiet contemplation for three days. A trial was held in which Captain Barros officiated. Gaston was numb and barely acknowledged the building of a rudimentary gallows, which consisted of a noose tied to a pole with a bench on which to stand while his sentence was executed.

At the direction of the Captains, Gaston was taken and stood upon the bench. He was found unanimously guilty at the trial. The testimony of Ferd was damning. The words they spoke were in Spanish, and Gaston understood little of it. But he could tell from the list of names of his victims that his crimes were numerous. Ferd had no reason to lie, and Gaston had no reason to doubt him.

To him, his life had been short. He had no memories prior to crawling out of the river less than a year ago. As the noose was placed around his neck, he looked to the heavens, and somehow he expected divine intervention. How could this be? Could he have done these things? White cottony clouds tumbled in the sky. Colorful birds flew overhead indifferent to the carnal actions of the men below. Captain Barros and Lorenzo stepped toward the bench on which he was standing and pushed it over with their feet. There was no long fall. The rope simply squeezed tight around his neck. He could no longer move air into his lungs. The dense green trees around the fort became a blur. He recalled how the light came to his eyes out of the darkness when he had crawled out of the river. The same light appeared, but was again, fading into black.

Chapter 2

Brock the Buzzard

Buzzards are a common sight in the southern United States[7]. In the South, there are two species, the turkey vulture[8] and the black vulture[9], and both are protected by the wildlife authorities. Over the years, the protection has boosted the population and reduced their fear of humans. Many would say they have become a nuisance, especially farmers, who say buzzards attack newly born calves by swarming them. Their awkwardness and general ugliness reduce their appeal, despite their needed role as a scavenger in the ecosystem. This strange tale is a true one about one particular black buzzard named "Brock."

One July morning I was checking fences along a ridge on a cow-calf operation in Tennessee. A summer storm had hit hard the night before, and the cattle fence was down in

---

[7] In North America a "buzzard" is a member of the *Cathartidae* family which is made up of vultures and condors. In Europe the term is used for members of the *Buteo* family which are winged raptors such as hawks, falcons, and eagles.

[8] *Cathartes aura*

[9] *Coragyps atratus*

several spots after being broken by fallen trees. The task was a pain and exhausting, and at noon I needed a lunch break. Setting upon one of the large limestone boulders along the ridge, I opened my paper sack and enjoyed a few crackers and summer sausage. The fence line ran in angular stretches around big oaks and hickories and the many limestone outcrops. The sky was now clear blue and cloudless. The grasses were waist-high and still wet from the rains. While squirrels barked at their recently weathered neighborhood, colorful songbirds chirped, and small brown sparrows tweeted while competing for the dropped seeds and worms surfacing from the soggy soil. Crows cawed from the treetops, and ever-present buzzards were making their circles in the sky.

While munching on the crackers and sausage, a movement at the base of the hill caught my attention. Making little noise through the damp leaves, a black buzzard was waddling around on the ground. I assumed he had discovered a small carrion unseen by his aerial comrades. However, as I watched him, he seemed to have no carcass but was slowly waddling up the hill. He was so far away from my vantage point atop the boulder I assumed he had not noticed me, though I was making plenty of noise. Nonetheless, he continued his slow waddle up the hill and came closer to my boulder. Within three minutes or so, he had come within ten feet of my lunch spot. "What are you doing, you ugly rascal?" I said. I assumed the words would startle him away, yet they had no effect. It paused for a moment, then continued to shuffle closer. Upon reaching the car-sized rock upon which I was lunching, he proceeded to climb up the far side with short, clumsy hops using the natural steps and crags of the stone to get to the top. He was now within three feet of me and sat down. "What is with you?" I said. Other than a casual look around and down the hill, he remained unbothered by my presence. I reached into my sack and retrieved a small rectangular club cracker. He watched me as I put it into my mouth and crunched it loudly. Taking out another one, he still held his ground with no apparent fear as I placed it near his feet. He turned his head sideways for a moment, then reached down and took the cracker in his mouth. It broke into a few pieces that fell onto the rock when he bit into it, but taking his time, he seemed to relish each piece, cleaning up all the remaining crumbs. Surprise turned to curiosity as I cut him off a piece of the summer sausage and laid it at his feet. Taking it into his beak, he chewed without hesitation, and swiftly gulped it down his featherless and wrinkled neck. Enjoying his company, I gave him a second piece and more crackers.

For a few minutes, I admired the unattractive yet friendly creature. When the lunch items were all gone, he continued to sit on the rock. "I've got to get back to this fence," I said before dismounting and resuming my task at hand. Looking back, the buzzard was still there. He watched me with only occasional looks down the hill and up at the tree canopy above. The hammering of fence staples into posts did not appear to bother him. As I moved several yards down the fence line to another damaged section, the buzzard dismounted and waddled closer to where I was. He found a section of dried log, stood upon it, and continued to watch. As I persisted along the damaged fence, his routine remained unchanged; when I moved a few yards away, he sauntered down the trail to find another boulder or limb to rest upon and watch me. "I don't have any more crackers buddy." I assumed that was what he was hoping.

By the end of the day, I had finished most of the repairs that needed to be done. "So long fella. I wish I had more crackers to give you, but I'm out. I'm headed home. You reckon I'll see you tomorrow?" As I began walking down the hill for the evening, the buzzard maintained his last perch and watched me descend the hill until we were out of sight of each other.

The next morning, I needed to check the remaining fence. As I saddled my horse, I wondered if the buzzard was still waddling along the ridge. I reasoned that the bird must have once been a pet. But whose? In such a remote spot, where could he have wandered from? Maybe there was something amiss with his ability to fly. Why did he have no natural fear of me?

I rode to a different section of fence, some distance from where I had been working the day before. I finished my work sooner this time, and I was curious if the buzzard was still where I departed from him yesterday. Having some daylight remaining, I rode over to the ridge where I had lunched with him previously. I had not even crossed the valley separating the ridges when I saw the wobbly buzzard coming toward me. As I approached, he showed no fear. I rode within twenty feet of him. He paused when I dismounted. I had some extra crackers and pieces of cheese in my saddlebags. The buzzard was happy to receive the vittles and devoured them as he had before. I stayed nearly an hour until the sun began its descent. He finished the crackers within a few minutes and spent the rest of the visit squatting on his haunches, looking at the horizon and occasionally over at me. As the day waned, I had to leave my feathered friend and head home for the evening. It would be a few days before I could come back, and I wondered if I would see him again. I worried about his risk of being eaten by the many coyotes that patrolled the hills at night.

Two days later, I received a phone call. It was from a friend named Brock. He told me he had finished some tractor work in the cow fields. "Oh, by the way," he mentioned. "Have you ever noticed a friendly buzzard back there?"

"I have actually," I said. "Did *you* meet him?"

"Yes. What's the matter with him?" he asked.

"I don't know, but he likes crackers."

Brock laughed.

I do not know why, but I started referring to the bird as "Brock's Buzzard." A few days later, I decided to take a ride up the hill to see if Brock's Buzzard was still up there. Indeed, he was. I got off my horse and walked up to him. "Hello

Brock," I said. He showed no fear as usual. The evening was pleasant, and I decided I would camp out there for the night. I built a small fire and spread out my bedroll. I sat upon my blanket, watching the fire and enjoying the calm company of "Brock" the buzzard. As the sun went down, Brock sat down on the blanket with me. He stared at the fire until it died down, then gazed up at the stars, just like I did. The sound of yipping coyotes caused him to look intensely at the direction of their sound when it pierced the darkness. In the morning, he was still there, sitting on the edge of the blanket.

At the light of dawn, I saddled my horse and rode back home, still thinking about Brock the buzzard. His kind and friendly nature, that shined through his ugliness, stayed on my mind. A few days later, Brock the farmhand, called back. He too, had been curious about the buzzard. I informed him that I named the buzzard "Brock" after him. He laughed with approval. He told me he spoke with a game expert, and they thought the bird was likely a juvenile and had not yet developed flight. Neither of us felt like this was the case. Brock, the buzzard, did not have the appearance of adolescence with his full size and plumage. The "expert" also suggested he might have a disease or have sustained an injury that robbed him of his ability to fly and scavenge naturally. He also said we should avoid contact with it. Why was the bird so apt to approach human visitors? Was it merely hunger that pushed him past the fear of humans? Hunger did not explain why he stayed by the fire, sitting on the blanket, long after the food stuffs were gone. We felt it was possible he had been someone's pet, but it just did not make sense for him to be there in such a remote location if that was the case.

I had occasion to ride the fence lines many times that summer. Regularly, Brock, the buzzard, was there. He never failed to be friendly and glad to accept the snacks I brought for him. Twice more, he camped next to me and seemed to enjoy the campfire and company as much as I did.

One evening in the fall, I discovered the inevitable. While riding across the valley, near where the second meeting occurred, I came across a pile of bloody vulture feathers. I was not certain at first, but after a closer examination of the carcass, I saw the familiar features of my friend. It was the earthly remains of Brock the buzzard. The coyotes had finally gotten him. I hoped it was not true, but after Brock was nowhere to be found, I knew it was – he was no more. I know it was the natural order of things, and the coyotes were just being coyotes, but Brock's death hit me like the loss of a friend.

An odd thing about Brock the buzzard was that even though he was eaten, people still saw him occasionally. During the winters, hunters reported seeing a large black bird walking toward them, but it would vanish as it got close. Even Brock, the fieldhand, told me he once saw him, but then he blinked, and it was gone. I had not told him that the buzzard had been eaten, and he was shocked when I did. He was nearly certain he had seen "Brock." "It had to be him. I'm certain it was him."

"Did he look any different?" I asked.

"It looked just like him; it had to be. I'll admit that he did look a little shinier."

"What do you mean?"

"It had to be him; he has a certain character about his face, you know."

"Yes, but what do you mean he was shinier?" I asked.

"Well, he looked kind of silvery."

I myself saw him. Twice I saw him moving toward me, but just like the others reported, he vanished as he got close. When I saw him, it was unmistakably him, but he did have a very sparkly sheen to him. The first time I saw Brock the buzzard after he was eaten was near the same valley where I had encountered him a few times and shared my lunch. The second time, I was camped not too far from the valley, trying to get a shot at a coyote or two. The coyotes had become so numerous on the ridge they were discouraging the hunters. When Brock appeared, I saw him walking toward the campfire. I even spoke to him. "Hey there fella!" I did notice that his appearance was more majestic. As previously mentioned, his feathers were silvery – not gray, but shined like metal reflecting the moonlight. Also, he did not waddle like before, instead, he moved very steadily, as if floating. Perhaps it was a figment of my wishful thinking, but as soon as I spoke to the bird, he vanished from right in front of my eyes.

Chapter 3

Quarantine of Knux Patterson

It is unknown when the virus that was to become the Spanish Flu made its initial leap into humankind. Nor who was its first victim. What is known is that the little viroid was able to sneak into the respiratory cells of humans, hijack cell's machinery, and create millions of copies of itself in a very short time. This is how influenza, as well as any other respiratory virus, is spread. The new viral copies are passed to a new victim, then to that victim's kin and friends. These new recipients become sick as their immune cells recognize the replicating virus as foreign and attack their own infected cells. This was how the Spanish Influenza made its way from person to person causing high fevers and cough. Some cases were mild, but other sufferers became severely ill. Many grew so sick that their lungs became inflamed and bacterial pathogens took advantage of the virally occupied respiratory immune cells; this usually resulted in death.

When this new influenza first made its way into humans, it might have smoldered along for years before there were enough sufferers to recognize a problem. However, in the beginning months of the Spanish Flu, the world was at war. The world order was thrown into disarray. Families were displaced into new countries. Refugees fled their homes and found safety in foreign lands. Soldiers were mobilized and moved by land and sea by the thousands. This unexpected reshuffling of humans around the world accommodated the potential of the virus. At first, its carnage went unnoticed among the violence of war, but soon the victims became so numerous they could not be ignored. Eventually, millions perished, and the Spanish Influenza claimed more lives than the war going on around it.

The Spanish Flu raged during the years 1918 and 1919. By 1920, it was beginning to diminish. Governments and communities implemented steps to mitigate the spread despite a minimal understanding of the disease. At the time, most people did not know the difference between a virus, a bacterium, or a demonic miasma. Many politicians were ridiculed for the way they handled the situation. They, in turn, were obligated to act more quickly and aggressively in the future. As a result, when officials learned of symptoms appearing in a community, strict quarantine was the solution. In this way, the spread of the virus was limited. By the winter of 1920, the spread of the Spanish Flu was slowing. The world was relieved by its retreat and had grown tired of the virus affecting their lives and stifling the joy of living.

Small pockets of influenza infections that resulted in community quarantines had become commonplace, to the point that small outbreaks were unnoticed by the newspapers. However, those in charge knew to act resolutely when the virus popped up. Those who were appointed to monitor the virus continued to be vigilant.

One such outbreak occurred in the small depot town of Bradshaw, Tennessee, when a particularly virulent strain of influenza found its way there. It was more deadly than some of the variants had been and certainly made its presence known. Bradshaw was little more than a handful of small businesses near a small loading dock on the L & N Railroad. One of the families that made up the population of the small town where the Pattersons. Knuckles Patterson and his wife Myrtle had two sons children and raised a few cows not far from the depot. Knuckles was known as "Knux" and also worked at a nearby sawmill to earn the family a little extra cash. Their small farm was located along Cottonwood lane, a small road that turned off of Main Street where the depot was located.

When Christmas came in 1920, all was well with the Pattersons. Cattle prices were up, so Knux took the opportunity to sell twenty steers, which was most of his herd. Work at the sawmill had been good. The owner of the sawmill, a man named Sturgil Melton, liked Knux because he was reliable, worked hard, and was courteous to the customers when they came in. Because of his kind and helpful nature at the mill, Mr. Melton gave him a raise just before the holidays.

Knux and the family were excited about Christmas. Times were getting better. The German Keiser had been defeated, and American soldiers were coming home. Businesses were doing well. The damned influenza was slowing down, and Knux had not heard of any new outbreaks in a few months. Selling the steers had brought in more than he expected, helping to ease his endless financial worries.

Myrtle and the children, Ladd and Knuckles Jr., were even more anxious for Christmas morning. Presents were piling up under the tree, and anticipation for what could be inside them abounded. It had been a long time since Knux felt this settled going into Christmas. He had a stack of wood that would last most of the winter. The money from the steers had enabled him to fill the smokehouse with beef, hams, and bacon. They had enough lard and flour to last until spring.

On Christmas Eve, snow was falling. It covered the grass of the cow pen, leaving the landscape clean and white. Icicles hung from the eaves from the house and barn, while inside, the warm smell of baking pies filled his senses. After taking a nap, he played a game of checkers with Knux Jr.

Christmas morning was a joy. The ribbon-bound presents under the tree contained shoes for everyone. There were also lots of peppermints and hard candies. The children received decks of cards and colorful paints. They also each received a pair of warm flannel pajamas. Knux enjoyed watching the family open their gifts even more than he enjoyed ordering them from the Montgomery Ward Catalogue. For the next two days, they played games and told jokes between wonderful meals of ham and roast prepared with love by Myrtle. Breakfast was bacon with apple pie and coffee. With their bellies full, Knux and the boys bundled up to go outside. The new shoes were stiff but warm. After giving the momma cows some hay, the boys built a snowman and pelted each other with snowballs until their fingers stung from wet mittens.

Knux and his two sons began walking down the road toward the depot which was not far away. He went to the depot regularly and usually ran into a friend or neighbor there. He enjoyed a good joke and liked to catch up on local happenings. He knew there would likely be no one there since it was Christmas and snowy. His main reason for going was to collect the day-old newspapers. There were usually discarded copies of The Tennessean or The Nashville Banner left by caboosemen on the lunch tables. Knux liked to read them and hoped to browse through them by the fire over the coming days.

Knux did not read well, but he was persistent at it. Myrtle liked to read poetry, but Knux could never get into the cadence of the lines. Myrtle also read the short poems in the newspapers Knux brought home. She tried some of the recipes and read some of the Bible stories and sermons to the boys.

Knux kept up with livestock prices and borrowed some of the jokes and funny stories near the editorials.

The main headlines these days were about the peace treaty in Europe and how things were sorting out in France and Germany. There were transcripts of speeches and obituaries of famous people who died. Updates regarding the Spanish Flu were also regularly featured.

That evening, sitting with his wool-socked feet elevated in front of the fire, a particular story in the paper caught his attention. "Myrtle, there is an article in here you ought to read."

"What's it about?" she asked.

"There has been some flu down around the state line."

"Near here?"

"That's what it says."

"Have you heard anything about it at the mill?"

"No, no one has said anything," he said.

"It has been a while since we have heard of anyone sick with it."

"Yes, it seemed like it was about gone."

Nothing more was said that evening. Myrtle finished her evening tasks in the kitchen while Knux read a few more articles in the paper. After a while, Knux went to bed, and Myrtle sat for a moment in his empty chair, feeling his warmth. She picked up the three-day-old copy of The Nashville Banner he had been reading. She read the article he was talking about. The headline said, "Deadly Flu Near the Alabama Border."

Bradshaw was only ten miles from the Alabama border, and Myrtle wondered how close this thing was to them. The date on the newspaper was December 23rd – a few days ago. The weather and the holidays had prevented in-person exchanges of news. If anyone had been sick lately, they would not have known about it. She put the paper aside and went to bed. The article read:

Deadly Flu Appears Near Alabama Line

It has been months since reports of an influenza quarantine have stricken the ears, but health officers have announced an especially potent strain has reared its head in small communities near the southern state line. Officials suggest a person unknowingly carrying the pestilence traveled along the L&N railroad line and likely disembarked at one of the small depot stops near the border. This likelihood is assumed due to the lack of other infected individuals in other parts of the state. Governor Albert Roberts has issued a statement. "Our lives continue to be interrupted by this vile influenza. Along with the rest of the world, our citizens have suffered its effects. In some aspects, our lives are returning to normal, yet we must persist in our vigilance against this unseen invader. We are beleaguered by its unrelenting assault on our families and communities, but our resolve is strong. We will do what we must to halt its spread and its path of death." Local constables have been tasked with the quarantine and hope to stimy the spread in days to come.

The week of the 27th of December began with a cool but sunny Monday. Mr. Vassar, the mailman, resumed his rural route in his four-wheeled mail carriage pulled by the aging gelding, Petros. Mr. Vassar loved Petros but was anxious to be issued a horseless Triumph motor carrier or even a Ford. Knux watched through the frosted windows to see Mr. Vassar pass the mailbox with no letters for them. He was enjoying some of the ham leftovers from the Christmas fixings when he heard a motor car coming down the driveway. He recognized the profile of the driver of the black Model T. Knux stopped his eating and watched Leon Schultz, a Lincoln County Sheriff's Deputy, step out of the car and close his coat against the cold as he walked toward the house.

"Leon! I'm surprised to see you out on such a cold day," said Knux as he welcomed him into the warm house.

"Thank you Knux. I'm sorry to bother you," said Leon.

"Not at all. What in the world can I do for you?" Myrtle heard the man enter and came into the sitting room to see Knux welcoming Leon. The deputy tipped his hat and acknowledged Myrtle.

"Well, I hope not to keep you long, but we got some folks with the fever up your road, and I want to ask about it."

"Really? Who is it?" asked Myrtle.

"It's the Binghams," said Leon

"Alice and George?" asked Myrtle.

"Yes," said Leon. "Their boy was in from his regiment for Christmas, and several in his unit have it, and now he has got Alice and George sick with it."

"That doesn't seem like big news," said Knux, "why all the fuss?"

"Well, this fever is especially bad. Most folks do not make it through," said Leon. Myrtle gasped as Leon continued. "There have been a few families eat-up with it, and most of them ain't makin' it."

Knux walked toward the fireplace and retrieved the newspaper he and Myrtle had been reading. He folded the paper to reveal the article about the virus. "Does it have anything to do with this?" asked Knux, pointing to the headline.

Leon had seen the article, as well as spoke with the health officer it mentioned regarding directing the quarantine. "I'm afraid so," he said.

"That's awful!" said Knux. "Thanks for letting us know. We will hold off on visiting 'till we hear otherwise."

"That is a good idea," said Leon, "in fact, it's a rule. The Governor's office is following this one, and they have a quarantine radius surrounding the folks that have it."

"A quarantine radius? What is that?" asked Knux.

"Well, that means you have to stay around your house until this all passes," explained Leon.

"Us?" asked Myrtle.

"Yep," replied Leon.

"That's a little much ain't it?" protested Knux.

"Yep, but those are the orders from the Governor's office."

"Well, who is going to enforce that?" Knux replied.

"The Sherriff's Office," said Leon firmly. Hoping to soften the feelings, he continued. "I realize this will be an inconvenience, but I will help if you need anything. Just get word to me, and it will be provided. Meat, milk, and the like. Just let me know." Knux sensed his sincerity and did not push the issue.

"Well, I reckon we have enough to make it through for a while," said Knux.

"I figured as much," said Leon, "but please don't hesitate to ask. Get word to me if you want for anything. I will be around every few days anyhow." Leon stood to walk out as the Pattersons struggled to say anything as they processed the consequences of Leon's news and instructions. "I wish you all the best, and I'm sure everything will resolve soon," Leon concluded.

"Thanks for letting us know," said Myrtle.

"Thank you for understanding, Mam."

"Stay warm Leon," Knux said as the deputy walked out of the house. "Oh yes, Leon, can you bring us some of the newspapers from the depot?"

"Sure will. I'll even do you one better. We get The Banner at the Sheriff's Office. I'll see to it that you get them."

"I hope that won't leave you without in the outhouse."

"We will make do," chuckled Leon.

Knux and Myrtle watched him get into the Model T and pull out of the driveway.

"Daddy, what was Leon doing here?" asked his oldest son, Knuckles Jr., coming in from outside.

"Apparently, the Binghams are sick, and we all got quarantined."

"Quarantined? What does that mean?" asked the son.

"It means we have got to stay around the house and not go to town or visiting anyone until it passes," said Knux.

"Who says?" asked the boy.

"The Governor," said Knux. With that, the boy was silent. He walked back outside to tell his younger brother.

The remaining days of the week passed uneventfully as Knux, Myrtle, Knuckles Jr., and Ladd looked forward to New Year's. Leon brought them no additional news, and Mr. Vassar, the mail carrier, had nothing to deliver as New Year's Day came and passed.

January 1st was on a Saturday, and on Monday the 3rd, Leon's car appeared in the driveway. It was an even colder day. Leon walked to the porch, and Knux let him in.

"Howdy Leon. Reckon things are getting settled," commented Knux. Leon looked grim.

"No, afraid not Knux. More folks are sick. The Bingham's neighbors, the Childers have it now," said Leon.

"Well, dang!" said Knux. "Are the Binghams mending?"

"No, they have gone," said Leon.

"Gone? You mean died?" asked Knux. Leon nodded to affirm. "Damn!"

"All of them?" asked Myrtle, beginning to cry. Again, Leon nodded. "Well help my time."

"The Governor's office says most folks don't make it that get this one," explained Leon. "I don't think y'all should get out for a while. In fact, is everyone feeling okay?"

"Yes!" said Knux. "We are fit as can be."

"Good to hear. Do you need anything?

"I don't reckon," said Knux. Leon handed Knux a bundle of newspapers he had collected from the previous days. "Anything in these about the quarantine?"

"Nothing that I saw," said Leon.

"Any word on when it will be over?"

"Not yet." Leon looked grim. "I'm sorry y'all have to endure this, but I think we will all be best off if we just stay put and avoid visiting."

"Well, that's just what we'll do."

"Okay then, y'all take care. I'll be in touch," said Leon as he stood and walked back out into the cold air.

Knux and Myrtle closed the door and sat in their chairs next to the fire. "Good Lord, Knux, how long is this going to last?" asked Myrtle.

"No tellin', Love. It could be a week or two, or it could be a month or more."

"Well, we've got nowhere to be. We can hold out a while."

"Yes, I'd say we will do best if we stay right here. We've got plenty of meat and flour," said Knux.

"You're right. We don't need anything." Myrtle kissed Knux on the forehead. "It's been nice all being here together. We're eating good. The boys like having you here instead of the sawmill. All in all, it's been fine." She paused for a moment. "It's awful about the Binghams though." Her eyes shone with tears. "You know Knux, that could have been us."

Knux stared blankly, acknowledging the reality that it could easily have been his family and how luck had graced them.

"I wish I could do something for them," said Myrtle. "I guess they are just lying there dead in their house with no one to go in and bury them."

"I don't think it will bother them that much, so maybe we shouldn't let it eat at us," said Knux.

"Will the same thing happen to the Childers?"

"To hear Leon tell it, no one makes it through."

Myrtle looked blankly at the wall, her mind racing with empathy. "I don't know Hattie Childers that well."

"Johnny Childers is a little odd. I see him at the sawmill every once in a while."

"How old are they?" asked Myrtle.

"I don't know for sure. I'd guess them both to be about fifty."

"They had a son. He's probably near thirty by now. I wonder if he knows?"

"I'm sure Leon or someone got word to him."

"Leon didn't say when he would be back, did he?"

"No, I expect it won't be until he hears something."

Myrtle went back into the kitchen while Knux settled in to reading the newspapers Leon brought. The coming days passed without any additional news. A week went by, and Leon had not returned. Mr. Vassar continued his mail route, but most days he passed by their mailbox without depositing any mail, only waving with a big smile.

Knux finished the newspapers Leon brought and wished for more. He wanted to walk to the depot, but orders were orders, so he stayed home. He thought about the Childers who had received the same orders but did not head them strongly enough and were likely going to die. This confirmed Knux's resolve to abide by the quarantine. Besides, the family was enduring few inconveniences. In fact, aside from the sadness from hearing about the Binghams and Childers, the family had enjoyed their time together. They were eating well, and everyone was cheerful. The boys were playful outside in the snow, warm-footed in their new shoes. They played games of rummy with their new decks of cards. Knux defended his winning record at checkers against Knux Jr. and Ladd, though not against Myrtle; she won with regularity. Knux justified midday naps, and Myrtle sang in the kitchen as she made her pies and studied the recipes from the newspapers.

It had been ten days since his last visit when Leon returned to the house. He looked grim as he got out of the car.

Knux opened the door to greet him. "Y'all doing okay?" Leon asked before getting too close.

"Fine as frog's hair," replied Knux. Leon walked closer. "How are things?"

"Not good."

"The Childers?"

"All gone."

Knux felt sick. Myrtle heard the words and reeled in horror.

"Anybody else Leon?" asked Myrtle.

"Yes," said Leon. "A few."

"Folks around here?" asked Knux.

"Yes."

"Who?" asked Myrtle.

Leon sighed before speaking, "The McLeods, the Stroms, the Brewsters." Knux turned pale. These were families he knew. These were their neighbors.

"How are they getting it Leon?" asked Knux. "Didn't they get the same quarantine orders as us?"

"Yep, but they still went to church. Two pews wiped out," said Leon. Myrtle could not speak. Peggy McLeod was her age. She had gone to school with her. Their children were the same ages. The thought of the McLeod's and the Brewster's children was a gut punch.

"Are they having funerals?" asked Knux.

"No," said Leon, "with their fireplaces out, their bodies will be frozen until spring."

"Spring?" shouted Knux.

"I'm afraid so," said Leon. "The fire department will come and torch the whole place when they get to it."

"With them still in there?" asked Myrtle.

Leon only nodded. He handed Knux a bundle of new newspapers he collected over the past few days. "There is nothing in these about the influenza, but it will still give you something to read."

"We appreciate it, Myrtle has been trying some of the recipes in the last stack, and that's been quite nice," said Knux.

"I hope it helps Knux. I know this is bound to be tough on you all, but if y'all can just stay locked away 'till this passes, I think you'll do just fine."

"Well, if the truth be known, Leon, we are having a pretty good time, other than the blues about the neighbors and all."

"Good to hear, Knux. Keep it up."

"We will, and thanks, Leon." Leon turned and walked back to his car.

"Knux, it's too much to think about those folks all dead and just lying there," said Myrtle.

"I know it's hard to believe."

"That can't be us. We have to see this quarantine through. They didn't take it seriously."

"We are gonna be fine. We know better, and we ain't going nowhere."

Myrtle walked into the house weeping from the news of the other families. A heavy gloom came upon them, where it had been joyous and happy. They resolved to heed the quarantine. They would not go out and certainly, would not let anyone in. He felt like those families were not much different than his. The virus was their enemy, and like him, they did not understand the enemy and how to fight it. He did know that they had to avoid contact with anyone. The others likely adhered to the restrictions of the quarantine but somehow felt the crowded church pews would be safe. They were not, and the assumption cost their lives.

That evening he got out his old banjo to lighten the mood. The boys' faces lit up when they saw Knux with his old instrument. He was not very good, but it did not matter to them, because he sang funny songs, and they knew they were in for a good chuckle. With loud il-tuned strums, he began *Oh Susanna*. The boys laughed and sang along. Myrtle came in to join them with a smile. They begged for another. He gave them an improvised version on *Commin' Round the Mountain*. "Daddy, play the one about 'the hole in her stocking,'" the boys begged.

"Oh, your momma hates that one," Knux said in jest. Myrtle laughed. "Okay, here it is." He sang –

Well, I danced with a girl with a hole in her stockin'.
Her heels were a rockin', while her knees were a knockin'.

Yes, I danced with a girl with a hole in her stockin'.
And we danced by the light of the moon!

Alabama gals won't you come out tonight,
come out tonight, come out tonight.
Alabama gals won't you come out tonight,
and we'll dance by the light of the moon.

The boys and Myrtle roared with laughter. "Another verse!" they cried.

Well, I danced with a girl with a wart on her chin.
Her knees turned out, and her toes turned in.
She was a purty good gal for the shape she was in.
And we danced by the light of the moon.

Alabama gals won't you come out tonight,
come out tonight, come out tonight.
Alabama gals won't you come out tonight,
and we'll dance by the light of the moon.

Myrtle's eyes watered with laughter, and the boy's sides ached from the hilarity. "Another one!" they demanded.

Well, I dance with a girl with some teeth in her mouth.
One pointed north, and the other pointed south.
Yes, I danced with a girl with some teeth in her mouth.
And we danced by the light of the moon!

Alabama gals won't you come out tonight,
come out tonight, come out tonight.
Alabama gals won't you come out tonight,
and we'll dance by the light of the moon.

With his banjo on his knee, Knux watched his family roll with laughter. Despite the recent shock of his neighbor's death, he could not recall ever being happier. Never had the family been closer or had more fun together. Quarantined in their small farmhouse with his family was the happiest they had ever been. They were warm, his job was certain to start back when the quarantine lifted, and they had enough provisions to last until spring. *What more could he want?* he thought.

The next morning Knux was sitting by a window in the living room. Looking out, he saw Mr. Vassar coming down the road. This time he stopped at the mailbox and put in an envelope. Mr. Vassar did not exhibit his friendly wave as usual. Rather, he bundled his collar around his neck and clicked for his horse to move on with the mail wagon. He shivered and coughed as the wagon began moving. Knux put on his shoes and walked out to the mailbox. It was a letter from Mr. Melton at the sawmill.

Dear Knux,

Leon told me about the quarantine. Seems like the damned flu won't quit. We are hoping to fire up the mill when you get back. Be safe, but hurry back.

Sturgil Melton

That was nice of him, thought Knux. He was restless to return to the mill and to resume the paychecks it provided. He was now experiencing some cabin fever. Knux put the letter in its envelope and both into his shirt pocket. He went out to see the cows and gave them a few bundles of hay. They appeared content chewing their cud.

The next day Knux spent most of it mending some walls in the barn to fight his restlessness. It felt good to use his muscles. He noticed that Mr. Vassar did not make his mail run today. He thought this rarity was quite odd. The day after, Knux's muscles were sore, and he found it harder to get out of bed than usual. His head ached. *I'm getting soft,* he thought. *One day's hard work, and I get sore.* As the day progressed, his achiness worsened. His nose began to run, and his throat hurt. *Well, that's what I get for working up a sweat in the cold weather.* He expected to be better the next day, but he was not. He now had a cough and hurt all over. Myrtle came into check on him. He was feverish. "Love, how are you feeling?" she asked.

"Not too well. I thought getting out and working on the barn would do me some good."

"You know Mr. Vassar did not run yesterday either," she added.

"He must be under the weather too," he said. Myrtle had an uneasy feeling, but she said nothing.

The next morning Myrtle also felt achy. She sat by the fire. The boys also felt unwell and had runny noses. Looking out the window, they saw someone putting something in the mailbox. It was not Mr. Vassar; it was Leon. She felt rough and was also developing a cough, but she put on her shoes and coat and went to the mailbox to retrieve what Leon put in there. It read:

Knux and Myrtle,

I wanted to let you know, Mr. Vassar the mail carrier, is very sick. Doc thinks it is the influenza. It looks like he won't make it. Stay inside and destroy any mail he may have delivered.

Yours,

Leon

Myrtle got Mr. Melton's letter out of the pocket of Knux's shirt that hung near the bed and pitched it into the fire. Fear gnawed in the pit of her stomach. She felt worse now, and their sons did too. They were in their bed sleeping, but coughing. Myrtle thought she would take the time to rest for an hour or so. She lay down next to Knux, hoping to awaken feeling better. She heard Knux's raspy breathing. His body was hot with fever. The fever was stirring wild dreams in his mind.

He dreamed he and his family were quarantined but were in a paradise. They were happy. They sang songs, laughed, and ate large feasts. He and Myrtle were enamored with each other and made love in a feather bed.

The dreams continued through the night. His fever was now high, and he no longer woke up between the dreams and hallucinations. He coughed, but it did not wake him. The next day, none of the Pattersons arose from their beds. Everyone coughed and smoldered with fever. Knux's fever reached such violent high peaks that he began to have febrile seizures. Myrtle was so near death that she did not awaken as her husband convulsed in her bed next to her.

Two days later, Leon pulled into the driveway of the Patterson's house. He did not receive the usual greeting of Knux from the front door. He stepped onto the porch and knocked – no answer. He knocked again, loud and long – no answer. He walked to the side of the house and looked into a window. It was the bedroom window of Knux and Myrtle. He saw them lying in there together, their breath still. Their faces were silent and gray. "Damn!" he said. He walked slowly back to his car. He was angry as he drove back to the office. "They caught it from Vassar," he grumbled to himself. Now the Pattersons were as dead as the old mailman.

Sitting in his office chair, he added the Patterson's address to the properties that must be given the torch in the spring. He was delivered the daily edition of The Nashville Banner. He thumbed through the pages. On page two was an article:

Influenza Strikes in Bradshaw

In the small town of Bradshaw, Tennessee, there has been a deadly outbreak of the influenza. The Governor's office saw to a quick quarantine before much spread occurred. A few families were affected, and there have been some deaths. The total number of casualties is unknown but estimated to be small. Governor Roberts issued a statement: "Our citizens have faced many challenges in recent years. We will face many more, and we will continue to show temperance and fortitude in the face of our adversities, just as the citizens of Bradshaw have shown. They are to be commended for their steadfastness and bravery. We pray for those who were lost and for those who remain."

Chapter 4

House on Fife Avenue

When I was in college, like many other students, I frequently accepted odd jobs to make ends meet. Though my emphasis of study would eventually change, it was then Animal Science. My goal in this degree was to earn the prerequisites required to apply to veterinary school. In addition, I hoped to learn more about the trade by working as a veterinary assistant, part-time, after classes. Working in this capacity enabled me to be introduced to all sorts of animals, large and small. Interestingly, the most enlightening component of this job was meeting the very interesting and peculiar characters who accompanied these pets during their visit to the vet. In fact, it was working as a "vet tech" and the human interactions that went with it that helped me change my decision and apply to medical school.

One particular duo I had the pleasure of meeting was R.J., a cat, and Francine Palmer, a southern lady. In his youth, R.J. was a large and proud orange-striped tomcat, but at twenty-seven years old, he was now arthritic, toothless, and incontinent. He had been neutered years before and became a lazy and friendly pet, and now required multiple different medicines to ameliorate his age-related ailments. Even as an old cat with crusty eyes and a sour expression, he remained a very friendly and likable creature who appreciated the care he was given. Francine found R.J. as a kitten when she was twenty. He accompanied her though her college years, through a few relationships, and through a number of "mid-life crises." R.J. had become an inseparable part of her life and identity. Francine never married and, at age forty-seven, was well established in her career as an accountant. She lived and worked in Fairdale, Kentucky, which is a picturesque town in the southern part of the state with many antebellum houses surrounded by green fields bordered by white fences. She still lived in the same house she grew up in. It was built in 1833 by her maternal sixth-great-grandfather and had remained in the family all these years. It had been a goal in her life to retain and live in it all of her days.

Her old house was simply beautiful. It was two stories with long windows and green shutters. Four white columns decorated the façade like bangs over a smiling face. It was adorned with furniture and artwork that her forebearers obtained and hung on the walls. There were two pianos and several old guitars that added a musical charm to the rooms. Each painting and wooden chair carried sentimental meaning as it reminded her of an ancestor or grandparent.

Francine frequently brought R.J. to the vet's office where I worked. His comfort and health as he grew older were her top priorities. It was not uncommon for her to leave R.J. with the veterinarian when she had to go on a trip because she knew he would be seen to and given his medicines properly in her absence. During one of R.J.'s regular visits, I was helping her with him as we waited for the vet to come into the exam room. Being a friendly and talkative person, she asked my name and if I was in school. I told her about my studies and that I was planning to become a veterinarian myself. She gave me a few words of encouragement, and the admonishment that my efforts would eventually pay off. She told me about her own college days and of all the places in the world she had seen. She also told me about her old house and what it meant to her. I was fascinated by the history she described. It sounded fascinating, and I told her I would like to see it sometime.

She was quite pleased with my apparent interest in old things and familiarity with architecture. She seemed to be pondering a question in her mind. After a moment, she said, "You know, it would be nice if someone like you could house-sit for me when I have to be out of town. You could keep an eye on the place and check on the old pipes if it gets cold. You would also be able to give R.J. his medicines. He would much rather stay at home when I'm away, but he has to have his medicines, so he stays here at the clinic."

I thought for a moment before saying, "I could probably do that."

The more *she* thought about the idea, the more it seemed practical to her. She continued, "In fact, it is a great place to study. There is an old desk in the big bedroom that is great for writing or working on term papers you might have, and great old chairs for reading. You would love sitting in front of the fireplace as much as R.J. does." Her sales pitch was working. I agreed it sounded like a great place to read and study, and seeing after R.J would not be difficult. I was comfortable giving him his medicines many times under the vet's guidance. Furthermore, I *did* have two term papers I was working on, as well as a test coming up for which I needed to study. I pictured myself reading by the fire and working on the papers on a regal old desk.

"All you would have to do would be to give R.J. his meds twice a day," she emphasized

"When is your next trip?" I asked.

"It is next week."

"I think I could be available."

"Perhaps you could come by this week, and I can show you around before you confirm." I accepted the invitation, as it was a great deal for both of us.

"I could come by this Thursday evening."

"That would be perfect. I'll see you then." Shortly after that, the veterinarian came in and chatted with Francine as he examined R.J.

"See you Thursday," said Francine as she put R.J in his carrier and left.

When Thursday came, I drove to her address. The house was set at the bottom of a hill at the end of Fife Ave. Fife was a small avenue connected to the town's square about a half-mile away. The lane had once been a delightful drive past old townhouses with beautiful gardens but now was lined with struggling and dilapidated storefronts and old pawn shops and gas stations. A pleasant rolling knoll separated the last crumbling brick building from the regal white house of Francine Palmer. The house was the last one at the end of the avenue that ended in a cul-de-sac. It was surrounded by tall oak trees and was certainly an inviting structure, kissed in sunlight and flocked with flowers in the yard and on the window sills. The front of the house conveyed the expression of a smile beckoning a visitor as I parked my pickup truck in the cul-de-sac. Birds sang in the tree above as I walked up the steps to the front door and knocked.

"Come on in," she said as she opened the door. "I'm so glad you decided to come."

"It's my pleasure, what a place you have," I said.

"Thank you. It's a wonderful old house, and so full of love and memories. Come on in, and I'll show you around."

I followed her through the ornate paneling and hardwood flooring of the foyer and into the large sitting parlor. A fireplace was lit, and a grand mirror with a gilded frame hung above the mantle. Beautiful old paintings of landscapes and watercolors of birds and flowers hung on other walls. A large claw-foot sofa sat in the middle of the room facing the fireplace and looked very comfortable. "This is the main parlor," she said. "Come this way, and I will show you the kitchen." The kitchen was tidy, and an old gas range with fine porcelain teacups was at the ready.

As we walked through the rooms, she told me about the various features of each room and which of her family members they had belonged to. In a room adjoining the square hall that led to a staircase was an especially beautiful bookshelf with four glass-paned doors. I noticed the bottom left door's glass was broken. "I see that broken glass door on the bookcase. That wouldn't be hard to replace."

She laughed and said, "That glass has been broken for sixty years. It's a funny story, and has become part of the history of the house."

"I bet you have a ton of stories like that."

"Indeed, the story of that bookcase is only one of many."

"What happened to it?" I asked.

"In the late 1930s, there were two traveling preachers visiting Fairdale. They put on a tent meeting one weekend. They drew a good crowd as preachers often did during those times. Well, after the sermon, the crowd began to dissipate, but no one had offered the two preachers a place to stay. There weren't many hotels then, and the one Fairdale had was full of folks coming to attend the tent meeting. My grandfather was in attendance that night and was talking business with some of the men after the crowd departed. The preachers came up to him and began hinting that they needed a place to stay. My grandfather did not want to bring them home, but his sense of politeness obliged him. You know what? It turns out those two preachers were swindlers, though no one in Fairdale knew it at the time. They supposedly got into a little bit of trouble in another town sometime later. Anyhow, they slept in this room. Grandma made them pallets on the floor, but they grumbled that they didn't get beds. I guess the house sensed they were no good because the two men said they got so hot they couldn't stand it, yet no one in the house felt anything out of the ordinary. The next morning grandpa walked in to greet the preachers as they were packing their things to leave. He noticed one of the glass doors of this bookshelf that then stood next to the window was broken. Red-faced, they told grandpa how it had gotten so hot in the room that they had tried to open a window, but it was so hot and humid that the wooden window's frame was swollen and wouldn't open. They tried to tough it out, but they couldn't stand it. To get some relief in the unrelentingly hot room, the two decided they would break the window, and the next day, apologize and have the window repaired. So, one of them threw a boot at the window in the dark. They heard the glass shatter, and immediately a breeze swirled in, and the room cooled down. However, the next morning, they awoke and in the light of day beheld the window they thought they had broken was still intact, and instead, the glass door of the bookshelf was broken." Francine laughed as she finished the unexplainable tale. "The preachers left and never came back to Fairdale."

She continued to tour through the house, introducing each room and each one's individual accoutrements. Lastly, she came to the "big downstairs bedroom." It was in the front of the house and its window, dressed with yellow curtains, was one of the large elegant ones seen on the front of the façade. Sunlight shone through the fabric, adding warmth to the visual effect of the room. The space also featured a small fireplace and rose and silver wallpaper which made elegant vertical lines from the chair railing to the twelve-foot ceilings. A silk rug was between the bed and the fireplace. This room also contained the mahogany desk she spoke of. It was positioned opposite the bed so that it received the radiant warmth of the fireplace. Its top was worn smooth from use, and a black leather chair that swiveled on coasters welcomed any writer to its use. "If you house-sit for me, you should sleep in this room. It is the most comfortable. You can read by the fire here or in the parlor, and this old desk is wonderful. Also, R.J. usually stays in this room, so you will be able to keep an eye on him. He doesn't do much these days other than lay around. He likes to stay close to the fireplace."

"Wow, Francine, how could I say no? The place is delightful and such a pleasure to the senses. You have kept it up beautifully. Each room has such character, and each one is so comfortable and inviting. It would be my pleasure to house-sit for you. I admit I have quite a few chapters I need to read, a test to study for, and two papers to finish. Seeing to R.J.'s medicine is no problem. I expect to be able to work quite productively here in your wonderful home."

"Oh, I'm so glad to hear. I think you will come to love this old place, just as much as I do. And, you will find, it will come to love you as well." I was not sure what she meant by saying the house would "come to love" me, nor was I sure of the odd smile she exhibited when saying it.

"I'm sure I will. Francine, you said your next trip was Tuesday, correct?"

"Yes, are you able to stay then?"

"Certainly, and thank you for the opportunity."

"You are quite welcome. I will see you then."

As she requested, I reported next Tuesday morning. She did not have long to exchange pleasantries as she needed to get to the airport.

"Okay, Hun, I've got to run. Thank you so much for doing this. R.J. will be so much happier getting to stay here. I'll see you on Friday."

"Absolutely! It's my pleasure. R.J. and I will be just fine. We are going to sit by the fire and read and work on papers."

"Great!" she said. "There are a couple of other kitties that come in through the pet door on the back porch. There is a big bag of cat food for everyone."

"Oh, okay," I said, surprised, as we had not discussed additional cats.

"Make yourself at home, and feel free to play the piano if you are of a mind to, R.J. likes it."

"I will do it," I said, and with that, she was out the door.

As soon as she closed the door, I felt a warm embrace of time in history in the now silent house. Clocks ticked on the wall as R.J. slid his old bony body against my leg before moving into the big bedroom to lie in his basket next to the fire. I followed him in with my suitcase of clothes and a satchel of books. Placing my case next to the bed, I set my books on the old desk. I then chose the old French barrel chair near the fireplace and, opening my Cellular Biology textbook, began to read. The crackle of the fire and the metronome of the ticking clock guided the pace of reading the text. It was very productive reading, and after an hour or so, I moved over to the desk to work on the term papers. My mind flowed with words at the desk. I quickly moved through the task of the writing assignment. I made few mistakes and, in the course of an hour, had made better than usual progress. When my hand grew tired of writing, I transitioned back to the chair by the fire for more reading. Aside from stopping to give R.J. his evening medicines, I continued in this manner without interruption until late in the evening.

By nine at night, my eyes had grown fatigued from the amount of material I was able to cover. To be fresh and prepared for tomorrow's classes, I needed to get some sleep, so I stoked up the fire and got into bed. The mattress was soft with a feathered top that was instantly a pleasure to rest upon. This action, however, triggered a response from the other cats. Four cats from outside bounded gleefully into the room as I pulled the soft quilts up to my chin. They were obviously participating in their usual routine of getting into bed with Francine when she retired for the evening.

I did not mind them getting onto the bed and would have welcomed their warmth and company during slumber, but to be still and snuggle was not their ambition. While I wanted to sleep, they wanted to grapple and wallow. They were not still for a single instant. Seeing they were only going to wrestle on the bed, I got up, put them out of the room, and closed the door. This had little effect. The latch of the doorknob did not catch completely. The old doorframe had warped just enough that the bolt of the door latch and its socket in the frame did not line up. The kitties were aware of this and simply pushed it open and returned to the bed.

While sweet old R.J. slumbered in his basket, his four young friends, whose names I did not know, continued their party. I resolved just to ignore them, but this was impossible. Their thrashing was too much. They were jumping on my legs and tickling my nose with their tails. It was getting late, and I had not been able to sleep at all. Tomorrow's classes would be difficult to endure if I was unable to get any sleep. Again, I got up and put the cats out of the room. To block their entrance,

I placed my shoes in front of the door so they could not push it open. This, too, did not last. The soles of the empty shoes made no purchase upon the hardwood floor, and with all four of them pushing on the door, they were able to open it enough to resume their trouncing upon the bed and tickling my face. I put them out a third time and put a chair in front of the door, certain this would prohibit their entering. No good. They leaped against the door, banging it loudly, and meowing until they moved the chair and resumed their disruption of my sleep.

This went on all night long. I arose the next morning tired and unrested. The classes were hard to endure in my un-slept condition. I was frustrated knowing tonight's studying and paper writing would be a struggle being so sleepy. I dreaded having to return to the house and endure another night of sleepless torture from the cats. When I pulled into the cul-de-sac, the house still wore its welcoming façade and invited me into its cushy chairs, warm fires, and superb desk; but inside, its cats awaited. I opened the door exhausted and dreaded an evening of forcing wakefulness during the evening's studenthood. The four cats who were so rowdy last night were now all sleeping on the back porch, spent from their night of ceaseless revelry. "You sons of bitches! Now you sleep?" I scolded them, but they remained completely indifferent to my complaints.

I ended my labors early due to tiredness. After giving R.J. his evening meds, I returned to bed. The cats were back in the room and on the bed before I even closed my eyes. *What am I going to do?* I thought. *This is impossible.* I got up and went into the parlor and lay down on the sofa, hoping the cats would stay in the bedroom. Useless. They instantly came into the large room and began to wrestle atop my legs. When I went back to bed, the cats followed. Anger filled my thoughts. *How can anyone sleep like this?*

"What am I going to do? Are *you* assholes going to keep me up all night, again? I said aloud. They continued their party. "This place is so wonderful, except for you jerks. I have to get some rest!" I lay still while they persisted, resolving to myself that another sleepless night lay ahead, but then something occurred. To this day, I cannot explain what happened next.

In the corner of the room opposite the desk, a presence manifested. It had no definite shape, and it first made no sound. The only visible part of what was there was the faintest scintillation of light that barely reflected into the corner where it appeared. I first thought my eyes were fooling me from the delirium of drowsiness, yet the slightest of perceptions of it remained. It began to move forward. I then made out the slightest sound of a boot's step coming from the corner, yet the sound was so faint I could not be certain I heard it. It continued to move toward the bed, and as it slowly advanced, it emitted a warmth as if a person was standing there, yet no one or thing *was* there.

A cold shiver of fear ran down my spine. What was this apparition before me? It was so implausible that I assumed I was hallucinating. However, the cats stopped their playful melee and looked at the blur as if it were familiar to them. A fleeting and barely perceptible arm reached forward and herded the cats from the bed. The cats obediently hopped off and walked calmly out of the room. The arm appeared again, reached, and closed the door behind them as they moved into the parlor. I was bewildered, it was as if the presence was empathetic toward my loss of sleep and was offering assistance. Curious, I stood up from the bed and walked toward the door. I opened it, and it creaked in its hinges. As I peered into the parlor, the glow was continuing across the room, guiding the cats in an orderly march out of the parlor and into the kitchen. On its way out, it passed the piano, and a flutter of air moved a few pages of sheet music that were arranged in front of the keys. Some of the keys were slightly pressed, and the piano tinkled with a few playful notes. The glow, and the cats, now moved through the kitchen and toward the back porch as I followed. The door of the porch opened, and the cats walked outside and resumed their playful tussling as the door closed behind them. I felt a wave of benevolence from whatever moved the cats outside and closed the door as if it cared for me and wanted to help me get a good night's sleep. Somehow, it knew I had been pushed beyond extreme weariness and wanted me to do well.

The cats did not come back into the house, and I slept like a baby. Francine's statement about the house showing love now made sense. The spirit of this kind old place was on my side and aiding my rest and comfort. The next morning, I felt refreshed and mentally alert. I attended the day's classes and afterward returned to the house on Fife Ave. that evening, finished the papers and continued my reading of the Cellular Biology text. The cats would not bother me that night, and I went on to do well on the test the following week. On Friday, Francine came home as expected. "How did it go?" she asked.

"It went great," I said. "The house is really a pleasant place to relax and study. I very much appreciate you letting me use it."

"Well, I'm glad. I can't tell you how many times this old place has watched out for me." After saying this, she stood and watched my expression curiously. I was sure she was wondering if I had experienced anything out of the ordinary. I looked back at her with a smirk, knowing the house's secret. She smiled back but did not say anything.

"Francine, it seems that the place has a benevolent presence that watches out for whoever sleeps under its roof."

She looked surprised. "Indeed, it does. I'm glad you were able to experience it."

"Have you ever seen anything odd at night?" I asked.

She smiled. "Yes, a few times, and not just at night. Did you?"

"I certainly did."

"Please tell me what you saw," she said.

"Well, I don't want you to think I'm crazy, but I saw something I can't explain."

"What was it?"

"It was something or someone. At first, it was just a feeling, but then a sort of shadow of a person appeared. If there was anything at all, it was barely visible." I told her about the cats and the sleepless first night.

She stared into my eyes intently as I told her the events of the second night. "That was Grandpa Carter," she said without hesitation.

"Grandpa Carter? Who is that?" I asked.

"He was my Great-great-grandfather, and was born in this house about a hundred years ago. He lived here all his life. I never met him, but he was supposedly very nice and all his grandchildren adored him. After he died, several members of the family, and occasionally visitors, saw his spirit visiting."

"So, you've experienced it to?"

"Yes, I first saw him when I was a little girl. I had heard stories from my aunts and grandmother. They said he would console crying babies at night, and close open windows if it got too cold; things like that, but I didn't believe it, until *I* saw him. I was about eight years old, and have seen him regularly since then. He is very kind, and sort of keeps an 'eye' on things, and is frequently helpful."

"Well, he certainly was, and I appreciated it."

Her eyes teared up as she said, "That's why I love this place so much. It takes care of me."

"It certainly does. Next time you see Grandpa Carter, please tell him, 'Thank you' for me."

"I will," she said.

Chapter 5

Little Nicholas

As a new physician, just out of training, I was elated to discover a small town in need of a pediatrician. Laurelton was a small rural city of four thousand people whose only pediatrician was retiring, leaving a thriving pediatric practice in need of a new provider. The town had a small, struggling hospital that managed a two-story medical office building that was only a decade old. The large red brick structure stood about one hundred yards away from the hospital and was built on a bit of property the hospital owned.

The plot of land had once been an old homestead, but all the remains of the original structures were long gone. A small clinic building had previously been constructed on the site, but the building had aged and been torn down, making way for the new large brick office building that could facilitate several medical practices. Dr. Miller, a pediatrician, had worked in the original clinic building for thirty years and then moved into a suite in the newer building, but after forty years of practice was ready to retire. Laurelton was quite picturesque and appealed to my rural preferences. It seemed like a perfect fit for me. After meeting the clinical staff, I felt I would do well there and was excited to sign the contract and move into the practice.

Dr. Miller took most of the artwork and room decorations with him when he left, so I was able to hang several art pieces I had collected on the welcoming walls. In addition, I had my diplomas, licenses, and board certification I was proud to display in the room that would become my office. In the waiting room and patient rooms, I hung the colorful paintings of horses, bears, moose, and other animals that bore friendly expressions on their faces. On my first day of seeing patients, the clinic looked cheerful and child-friendly. The children loved the funny paintings, and it offered a bit of whimsical relief to them as they got their vaccines or had their ailments addressed.

Anyone who has hung a picture on the wall knows that getting it to hang straight requires a little adjustment. Usually, after you hang it up, you make it as level as possible, and then after a few hours, the wire hanger on the back, settles, and you straighten it up again. It normally does not take much adjustment after that to make it hang straight. That was not the case in this building. Perhaps it was because the building was so close to the new four-lane highway, and the large trucks that rattled the ground vibrated the foundation. Or maybe, it was the frequent closing of the large wooden doors of the exam rooms, causing the walls to shake. The nurses thought it was from the children bumping the walls as they waited to be seen. None of the reasons proposed seemed to fit, and other suites in the building did not have this curious issue. Whatever the cause, the framed hangings would not stay straight. More precisely, they would stay straight when they were adjusted in the morning, and throughout the day, but overnight they would shift and be crooked again the next morning. Even the diplomas on my office walls would be unlevel.

Crooked pictures on the office wall were not the only things we noticed. In the mornings, when the first person entered the office for the day, they would frequently find pencils or crayons lying on the floor and arranged into shapes. Also, toys and magazines in the waiting room would be moved and placed like action figures into a playful scene. The cleaning ladies said they saw no pencils, crayons, or toys in odd positions before they left in the evenings. We had no explanation. A couple of years went by, and the practice thrived. However, even after two years, the wall hangings continued to be crooked in the mornings. The re-leveling of the frames became a fun part of the morning opening routine, often with jokes about ghosts or night pranksters as the culprits.

I felt lucky to have moved into such a wonderful community, where everyone I met was welcoming. They also liked to have a good time and had great agricultural festivals such as tractor pulls and livestock shows. One such festival was the annual Rabbit Festival, which they still host after over fifty years. Folks from all around the world come to enjoy the event.

There are rabbit shows, rabbit pageants, rabbit plays, and just about every form of rabbitry one can imagine. In addition, the attendees tend to dress as rabbits, and the event has evolved into a giant rabbit party. Much like a county fair, various businesses set up booths to show off their services, even if they have nothing to do with rabbits. Car dealers, hardware stores, and banks are just a few of the businesses that send representatives to chat up the Rabbit Festival fans.

The first time I attended the festival, I thought it would be a good idea to go in my lab coat blazoned with "pediatrics" and hand out business cards. It was a fruitful idea since there were lots of families with children there, and many of them were looking for a fun-loving pediatrician. I introduced myself and shook hands with hundreds of parents enjoying the festivities. I enjoyed it very much, but as the day went on, I grew quite tired, and my feet were killing me from having been socializing on the pavement of the fairgrounds. Looking for a place to rest a moment, I spied a shaded bench next to one of the livestock pavilions which was currently inhabited by several dozen prized rabbits and their proud owners. It felt great to take a load off and relax on the bench amidst the good time being had by all.

A gray-haired lady with a walking cane also saw the shady spot where I sat, and with the help of her granddaughter, made her way over to join me. Just like me, she was sore footed and wanted to rest for a few minutes.

"Here you go Granny," said the helpful granddaughter, "Steve and I will be right over here if you need anything."

"This is fine my dear," she said. "I'll just sit here for a bit. You go and have fun."

"Okay Granny. I gotta go wrangle these kids." The kind old lady waved as her granddaughter walked back toward her two daughters running to and fro among the friendly crowd. I turned and smiled with a nod, and she smiled back.

"You are the new pediatrician in town, aren't you?"

"Indeed I am, and it's a pleasure to meet you."

"I tell you, I have been coming to this Rabbit Festival for years. It gets bigger every year, and I love it, but each year it gets harder for me to get around."

"I would say so, but it seems like you are still managing quite well."

"Oh, thank you for saying so. My name is Sally Goforth."

"Well, Ms. Goforth, it's good to make your acquaintance."

"Thank you, but please call me Sally."

"Okay, Sally, I'm Bill."

"Bill, I'm sure you will do quite well in Laurelton. Children respond so well to a friendly face."

"Wow, thank you for saying so. I see *your* family is with you."

"Yes indeed. That was my granddaughter just now, but she has her hands full with her own wild ones. Nine-year-old twins! I hate to be a burden to them, but it has become a family tradition to attend the Rabbit Festival. The girls are to be in the Little Miss Rabbit Festival Pageant and Parade."

"Well, it looks like they are having a wonderful time."

"Oh yes, quite a good time. I can't keep up with them. Tell me young man, how is your practice going?"

"It's going very well. We have continued to grow and have become quite busy."

"Oh, that's wonderful. I knew Dr. Miller, who had the practice before you. Did you know him?"

"I met him once, but I didn't know him well. He was ready to retire and move on to his next phase in life when I met him."

"He moved to Florida, did he not?"

"Yes ma'am, he did."

"He was certainly a nice man, but I don't know what is in Florida that would make him want to move there."

"Sun and sand, I think."

"Yes, I bet you're right, but I say 'no thanks.'"

"I agree. I prefer the green hills."

"As do I," she said.

"Laurelton is certainly a nice place. I love it here."

"Good to hear. The town has lots of young families that need a good pediatrician that cares about them. All of my family loved Dr. Miller. I'm sure they will become fond of you as well."

"Thank you."

"You are in the upstairs of the new office building, is that correct?"

"Yes I am."

"Is the suite you are in nice, and suiting your needs?"

"Oh, very much so."

"That's good. I still remember the old clinic building that Dr. Miller used for years, but it was quickly getting decrepit before they tore it down."

"I'm sure it had lots of stories to tell," I said.

"Indeed, it did. Do *you* ever hear from Little Nicholas?"

"I'm not sure I know who you are referring to."

She laughed, "Little Nicholas hung around the old clinic building and tinkered with things at night."

"Oh wow! That can't be good. Did he have parents?"

"Yes, but Little Nicholas died."

"Oh, that's terrible."

"Yes it was, but have you ever heard of the story?"

"No, I have not."

"Well then, I must tell you."

"Please do."

"Well, you see, long before the hospital was built, the land where it is now was all farmland. A few different families lived on the farms and worked the fields. One of the families, however, had a house that sat just behind where the old clinic would be built. In fact, their barn sat on the very spot where they built it, and where the new brick building now stands. The old barn was a typical barn and nothing fancy to speak of. The family to which the barn belonged had several children, and the youngest was named Nicholas."

"Do you recall their last name?"

"No, I can't remember their last name, you know my memory isn't what it used to be, and I haven't heard anyone speak of them in years, but they used to be talked about aplenty. You see, Nicholas fell out of the barn loft and was killed.

"Oh! That's terrible!"

"Yes, it was one of those community tragedies that everyone felt. The family was a nice bunch and loved by all, and their little Nicholas was an especially handsome boy. He was probably five or six when it happened. Apparently, he loved to play in the barn, and would cry and act out whenever he had to come into the house at night. He'd rather have just kept playing in the barn, bless his heart. They said he was so cute playing his pretend games at the barn, he pretended it was his castle, and other children loved to come to play with him. He didn't cause too much trouble while he was out there, but could be a bit of a rascal when he came inside. So, to keep him happy, and out of mischief, they let him play out in the barn most of the day. Children *now,* of course, aren't allowed to play alone, folks worry too much."

"And rightfully so."

"Indeed, but then it was normal. Well, as you can predict, the inevitable happened. One day while playing in the loft, he was swinging on a rope he tied to the rafters and fell out of the loft. He hit his head and died just a few minutes later. The family was devastated, and never completely emotionally recovered. As time went by, the family still grieved but noticed strange things happening around the farm."

"What sort of *things*?"

"Hearing laughter coming from the barn's loft at night, and various tools being moved from where they had been put away. And sometimes, little toys and baubles, like a child would have made, were found in the middle of the loft floor. Rumors began to spread that the ghost of Little Nicholas was still playing up in the barn. Of course, I don't believe in ghosts, and many don't, but nonetheless, the story spread."

"Well, folks do love a good ghost story."

She laughed in agreement. "Years went by, and the family continued to experience odd things around the farm and hear things at night. Perhaps it gave them comfort to think of his spirit still playing among them. I guess in a way they liked having him around."

"What became of the family?"

"Eventually, the older remaining children moved away, and the mourning parents grew old as well. After the parents died, the family sold the farm to a developer, and sometime later the original hospital was built. Of course, that first hospital was torn down after several years, and the new larger one was built in its place. A few years later, Dr. Grange built the clinic building that Dr. Miller would eventually move into. It was just before Dr. Miller moved in that *I* first heard of Little Nicholas. The nurses in Dr. Grange's office said the pictures in the clinic would not hang straight."

Mention of the pictures startled me. "What do you mean, 'they wouldn't hang straight?'"

"They would level them in the evenings, but the following morning they would be crooked again."

"Would you believe me if I told you, I've noticed the same thing?"

"I don't doubt it. After Dr. Miller took over the practice, he and his staff noticed the same things happening in the night. They also said items from the office would be moved occasionally while they were gone. Nothing stolen, just toyed with. I never heard if the odd things continued to happen after they tore down the old clinic and built the new one. So that's why I asked, if you had heard from Little Nicholas."

"Well, in that case, I guess I have," I said.

"Hey Granny, the pageant is starting in a few minutes, you wanna go with us?" asked her granddaughter coming back to check on her.

"Yes, I guess I will," she replied, "Bill it was great talking with you, and do say 'hi' to Little Nicholas for me."

"It was an absolute pleasure to meet you, Sally. You have certainly explained a few *things* I've discovered. Thank you." The patient granddaughter helped her up and hugging her arm, walked with her toward the bandstand.

I decided to go by the clinic on my way home. It would be empty and I wanted to look around after hearing Sally Goforth's story. Unlocking the door, all was silent. The pictures still hung straight and had not yet been made crooked. "Nicholas," I said, "I hope you enjoy the new decorations of the clinic, and it is to your liking, enjoy the toys. If there is anything you need, please let me know. I'm sorry about what happened to you, and I hope you are able to find happiness. I'm going to head out, but will be back tomorrow." As I turned around to walk back out of the door and lock up, I nearly stepped on the collection of wooden blocks in the waiting room. They had been moved in front of the door and were not there when I came in, and were arranged into the shape of a heart. "Very nice, Nicholas. I hope we have a fun time together here." I squatted down and arranged the blocks into the shape of a smiling face and said, "good night, Nick." I left and locked the door behind me.

The next morning the pictures were crooked as expected, but the blocks had been rearranged into an "N."

Chapter 6

Beatrice

Beatrice Frank was sure she made the right decision. The oak door of her new cabin squeaked in its hinges as she pushed it open. The sound was a welcoming "hello." The door was heavy and adorned with decorative iron plates and rivets. She ran her fingers along the grain of the boards, whispering "my little castle in the woods" to herself. When she first saw the listing of the cabin for sale, she knew instantly it would be the setting for a new and final start. It was a hidden place. A veiled fortress in the wilderness she hoped would shelter her from further calamity. If the quaint square cabin could not provide this safety, nothing could. The photographs in the advertisement offered an unpretentious "tin-roof cabin in secluded backwoods of exceptional beauty." It satisfied an ever-growing plea from inside her to endeavor at least once more at something entirely dissimilar from her past. It was perfect. It would protect and distract her from the memories of her once-beloved city, which now cruelly and relentlessly reminded her of her absent friends and family.

A year ago, she was a middle-aged woman and recently widowed. The death of her husband drained her emotionally and physically. Their marriage was happy until his sudden illness spiraled rapidly into the inevitable. Though emotionally beleaguered, she accomplished a degree of healing with the support of her close friends. Her two best friends helped her the most with constant encouragement and love, partially filling the void in her heart with happiness. The death of those two friends in a fiery car crash while on their way to visit her deepened an emptiness that subsumed any expectancy of joy. In her lowest hours, she yearned to join them and to share their condition. She envied their freedom from sadness and desired their state of nothingness. Yet faintly flickering in her bleak darkness, a small and imploring utterance within in her could be heard. From somewhere in her soul came a primordial compulsion to resist defeat. Its clamoring could barely be heard among her internal cries of loneliness, but with what remaining strength she had, she endeavored to rally to its very last charge. She would make one last attempt to leap free from her depression's engulfing abyss.

Her new little cabin was indeed the opposite of the city life she wanted to leave. In the busy city, new friends were everywhere to be found and were just an introduction away. She dreaded new introductions now. To become attached to a new friend meant a risk of losing them, and recently those risks had manifested too frequently. Her emotional vault was empty, and she had no reserve to pay the eventual emotional cost their loss would bring. The cabin's solitude would prevent that from reoccurring.

The dense trees surrounding the cabin were an armor of green that guarded her against the unfamiliar. She desired emotionless quiet so she could find a work to lend her passion. That work now would be to write stories that swirled in her mind that were to be captured onto the page. But more than anything, she hoped to find a way to unshackle the happiness she once knew, and enjoy the bliss her new surroundings would bring her.

On the drive down to her new abode, she exited the interstate and turned onto highways where the sky was released from its confines. The highways narrowed into rural roads that lead her to her inviting and enduring new home in the country. The gentle rattle of gravel under the Subaru Outback and rented U-Haul warmly welcomed her as she turned onto the road that ended at her cabin. What she beheld was beautiful and endless. She had answered the silent summons to persist. It was hers!

In the center of the cabin was an open table. It wasn't beautiful or valuable but was lovably worn. It beckoned for her to sit and write. The table was illuminated by the natural light that came freely into the windows on every side of the square structure. At night, a warm glow from the milk glass fixture above continued the invitation through the night. She stood an easel next to one of the windows. When the weather was nice, she placed it on the large covered porch just outside the door. She brought no photographs or images that would remind her of lost friends. In their place, she painted new ones – faceless landscapes of simple colors.

The little log house sat in the middle of a valley accessible only by the gravel road. Within a stone's throw around the back half of the cabin was a creek that carved a deep crevasse through the rock that supported the great dense wilderness which rose steeply from its banks. She stared down at the water and heard its trickling whispers, telling her it was alive and there for her. It introduced her to the deep dark woods on the other side, revealing its gentleness. For as far as she could see, the great trunks of hardwoods lifted an impenetrable canopy, like the arms of a steady lover. They held them up, not only for her but for the other small creatures who lived there and sang to her in the night.

Her first nights at the cabin were among the most peaceful she had ever experienced. The days likewise were filled with naps and peaceful strolls through the spaces of the hardwood trees. She explored these woods as if courting a lover. Could they be as kind and resilient as they seemed? The night sounds were beautiful. She stayed up late listening to them, and wondered what pleasant critters made them.

The first gray day did not come until she had been there a week. The dimmer light slightly modified her new routine of walking. The lights inside flickered as the wind picked up and wiggled the wires outside in their crusty connections. The drizzle of rain in the evening changed the songs that came from the dark wood. She opened the door of the cabin and listened to the long call of a lone birds. Its passionate pronouncement cut through the air while the other crawling minstrels sheltering from the dampness were silent.

She heard the deep hoot of an owl coming from across the creek where the steepness of its forming rocks made it difficult to cross. "Perhaps Mr. Owl is shy like her and doesn't come out often," she thought. As the night continued, the rain increased and was announced by distant thunder. This seemed to enliven the owl, who was now calling more frequently with a playful monkey-like chatter as if to draw her outside. She closed the door and sat down at the table. Lightning now preceded thunderclaps. Her bare toes curled into the fibers of the rug beneath her.

To distract from the startles of close lightning and its crushing thunder, she held her pen in hand with hopes of finding poetic words inspired by the torrent outside. She relaxed, knowing the storm would not breach the walls of her castle that had withstood much worse.

After an hour, her tablet was still blank, but her third wineglass was empty. She listened to the storm pass as the wine brought its warmth. As the volume of the thunder relented and the lightning became distant, the rain stopped, and the sudden stillness drew her outside. The sky was black and a curtain of storm clouds hung between her and the moon. The distant lightning momentarily illuminated an angry churning sky that reflected a faint green.

She knew it was harmless but felt its appearance ominous. She watched the churning pillows grapple in the gray heavens, which only a day ago were the brightest blue. She walked several steps into the space between the trees and the covered porch. Barely visible through the trees, she could see the darkened clouds and violence of the lightning sprouting. There were clouds and more lighting in the distance churning toward her indicating more storming to come. She watched a few moments more, waiting for the rain to start again.

Not far from her in the trees above came the sound of hooting and cackling from the owl she heard earlier. It was close. Why was this crazy owl so rambunctious all of a sudden? "Why are you not hunkered down for this storm?" she said. Her eyes searched the highest branches above her, looking for this noisy owl. She took more steps away from the porch light to look for him but saw nothing. "Odd fellow," she chuckled.

Craving the warmth of her quilt and flannel nightgown, she decided to postpone her admiration of her secluded paradise to a brighter day. She turned to walk back into the cabin when she heard wings flapping behind her. She reflexively crouched to the ground and quickly turned to catch a glimpse of a winged thing passing over her head and into the darkness. "The owl! Dang, that crazy thing!" she said aloud. The creature made an arch in flight and came back toward her. As it neared, she beheld his round face heading straight to her.

She saw a dim shattered reflection in its eyes and became horrified by the bird's expression. Its eyes were dead and absent. Was it flying at her just to torment her? Beatrice screamed and ran toward the porch. Reaching the door, she opened it and ran inside. She turned and looked through the slit of the partially open door. She saw the crazy owl make one more curving flight past the porch then ascend into its realm above to continue its cackling.

The behavior of the owl annoyed her. What an obnoxious thing to have to share the woods with. Was this its typical reaction to a stormy night in the summer? It had startled her, and she didn't like it. It was the first fright she had experienced since coming. She closed her eyes and breathed deeply, hoping to make the feeling pass hastily. She relaxed, reminding herself of the storm's inability to harm her, and of the strength of the log walls around her. Sleep was difficult that night, from the noise outside and the thoughts of the owl, and what an annoyance to have the thing flying at her when she walks outside.

The storm raged as she lay still in bed. Wind whistled through the usually silent walls. The rain roared against the roof and the broad green leaves outside her windows. The noises of the walls were occasionally musical through its swells and decrescendos. Some of the sounds were lively, while others were long and angry. Suddenly a noise overcame the sound of the storm. She dismissed it from the chaos the first time she perceived it, but the second time it came, it was undeniable. It seemed like a deep voice howling in the distance. It couldn't be. She tried to dismiss it as a random sound made by the wind, but it continued to come. Surely it was just the wind. It frightened her. It sounded like it was saying her name. Screaming her name. The distant howl seemed closer as it continued. "Bea! Bea!" It couldn't be. Maybe it was shouting something else. She forced herself to overcome the startle and convinced herself it was just the wind, but the voice continued. She was certain she heard it say, "Bea! Bea!" The sound eventually stopped as the fury of the storm rose. When she no longer heard the cries, she calmed a little and declined the assumption it was human and that it was calling her name. She closed her eyes to submit to what sleep would be available despite the continual booms of thunder.

When morning came, she hurt. The night of agitation yielded no rest and had bullied and robbed her of restful stillness. A tremendous clap of thunder brought more alertness. The rain relented but was still rattling upon the roof. There was no morning sun to light her way to the table. She made coffee under the electric bulb, which she had not done before. She stretched her arms and legs while the coffee brewed to work out the stiffness from the restless night. The smell of the coffee was the first pleasantry of the morning. She wanted to make the most of this rainy day, and planned to cozy up at the oaken table with her pad and pencil.

She poured a cup and held it under her nose. Breathing in the warmth of the coffee, she ambled in temporary bliss toward the door to look out its window. The aroma of the first sip produced its intended enlivenment. She blinked her eyes firmly to clear her vision of the tempest outside.

The visible trees were bent under a gust of wind. Returning upright only momentarily, they seemed perturbed and began flailing their limbs again when the wind sent another stronger blast. Flashes among the clouds revealed the sheen of the saturated ground. She could not see the water of the creek because of the steepness of the ravine through which it coursed, but she was sure its level was up. There was no sign of the owl. She was glad. Perhaps later in the day, she would put on her parka and walk around outside if the rain let up.

She stepped back from the window of the door, the next sip of coffee having a similar effect to the first. She leaned back to stretch the muscles of her back and felt them loosen a little. Feeling slightly better, she moved toward the square window near the door to better look at the porch and the rain coming off of the cabin. With the curtains pulled back, she could see the streams of water flowing in fingers out of the crimps and bends of the roof's metal overhang. She leaned forward and turned her head toward the rafters. No big leaks. Her eyes scanned the dark corners of the porch roof. The metal was solid. She bent her head to see the final dark corner, which was not as easily seen as the others. Her eyes focused on the structures and their shadowed corner. Something was blocking it. The owl! There he was! "Damn!" she sighed.

The owl was making no sound or movement. His face was turned toward hers, and she could see its oddly blank eyes fixed perfectly still. Frustration swelled within her. She was annoyed; not just at the owl, but that the cabin was not as warm and pleasant this morning. She was dissatisfied and uncomfortable. She had previously awakened to pleasant dawns, and the niceness of the morning had prompted a new and satisfying routine. This was not the case today. For the first time, she was not snug and cozy in her new home. This morning, the house nor the woods were the charming lovers who greeted her upon awakening.

She tried her best to ignore the storm, and the owl perched in her porch rafters, while the increasing wind flung all manner of sticks and limbs against the roof. To tame the roar of the rain and the plinking of hail, she turned on her old Magnavox record player. She lay the needle onto the spinning Patsy Cline vinyl and turned up the volume. Now at this table, she was warm and dry in her red gown while the storm had its say outside. She sipped her coffee and readied her pencil at the pad. She sighed in comfort as she overcame the fear of the storm. It could not hurt her. The walls of the cabin were solid, and that gave her comfort.

It was a few minutes after noon, but lightless enough that she required the electric lights. After tucking the collar of her gown snugly around her neck, she put pencil to paper. At the same moment, a flash of lightning with its instant cannon's fire of thunder struck something nearby. It left her ears ringing and rendered the cabin dark and silent in an instant. The sounds of the storm outside filled her ears. The crack of lightning and sudden power outage made her scream. "Damn this day!" She worked to calm herself and reasoned the electricity would come back on in a moment. Holding back her tears in defiance, she stood and began feeling around for a flashlight. There was one in the kitchen. She turned and moved toward the drawers next to the sink. The silence inside the cabin only emphasized the noises of flying debris hitting the wall outside. The rain on the metal roof grew deafening as the sheets of water moved like fringe and pounded its rhythm on the roof. She continued to shuffle her feet toward the drawer when a large gust of wind whistled through the log walls. This was followed by a deep crunching she felt in the ground beneath her. The crunching was deep and strong.

She was opening a drawer and feeling for the flashlight with trembling fingers when a corner of the cabin suddenly imploded toward her. A shower of wet glass and boards knocked her backward. She perceived that a massive something had just crashed through the roof. A coarse wet branch and its leaves scraped across her face and nose. She screamed and grabbed her stinging brow as a spray of water soaked her face, making her cough. A great hole in the roof allowed the rain to pour directly on her.

She shook in terror trying to catch her breath. She screamed again then froze trying to make sense of what happened. The thing that hit her in the face felt like a tree limb, so she assumed a tree had fallen onto the cabin. The blast had overturned the oaken table and its chair. The table was lying on her legs, but she was able to wriggle from under it. Rain stung her face as her eyes adjusted to the darkness. She tried to assess what part of the cabin had been crushed and what was left, making out part of the great tree which had fallen and smashed a corner of the cabin. Once on her feet, she moved into a section of the room that was still intact. Clearing the rain from her eyes, she was able to make more sense of what happened.

The tears came now. The cabin was no longer her protector. One of its walls was crumpled. "Damn it!" she screamed with fury. She continued to fight it, but fear was overcoming her. Suppressing her crying, she thought about what to do next. The counter was smashed. The flashlight was under that tree somewhere. She thought it best to feel for the door. When she found it in the dark, she could tell the frame around it had collapsed and would not open. Her next thought was to move back over to the dry corner from whence she came. Carefully, with socked feet, one in front of the other, she felt her way through the broken glass and around the fractured ceiling boards.

Tears impeded her vision. She wiped her face on the wet sleeve of her gown. With the white lace of the other sleeve, she cleaned the clear snot from her nose. The frequent lightning gave flashing images of the colossal tree. Drops of rain sparkled like diamonds thrown by an angry god from the ever-present clusters of lightning. Movement caught her eye. Amidst the flashes, a pair of wings appeared overhead. Her heart pounded. The flapping wings came in through the hole in the roof. Once inside, it extended its legs and lit on the great trunk of the tree now lying horizontally in her kitchen.

"Get out!" Anger mixed with terror as she reached to grab what loose thing might be next to her. A tapered portion of a ceiling plank found her hand. She could lift it. She stood and flung it with all her might. "Get out!" she cried again. The plank went over the owl's head, and the odd beast moved two steps to the left, his dead gaze fixed in her direction. "Leave me alone!" The owl spread his wings and stretched his head toward her. She yelped as he leaned into flight toward her. In horror, she fell to the floor, swinging at the darkness. She felt sharp stings on her head and the weight of something settling upon it. She swung her arm and felt the smooth wet feathered body absorb the blow only to take another purchase into her scalp. In vain, she tried to shake loose from its awful claws. He only changed his grip from her scalp to her brow and the bridge of her nose. It flapped its wings and pulled at the hair on her head with its curved beak. She felt the stinging pierce of the talons in her forehead as they climbed back onto the pole of her head and gripped. She shook with terror. With the bird on her head, she clenched her fist and punched the flailing attacker. The punch landed and sent the owl into the darkness. She pulled back for a second swing for his expected return, but it never came. "Get out!" Her voice shook as tears flowed.

What had happened? In a matter of seconds, the structures she escaped to for protection were crumbled. The cabin had turned against her. The great oaks outside the cabin were no longer steadfast centurions. Now they were threatening to fall.

The sound of wings beating rapidly against the floor appeared. It was in flight again! She screamed and clenched her fists, ready for it to come back. Instead, it took rest upon the large oak again. "Get out!"

The owl's head turned on its axis, yet its eyes saw nothing. He leaned forward into the air again to perch on her head. She bellowed and swung her fists at him. His path of flight missed her head, and he turned back for her in the empty space of the cabin. There was no way out. The door was jammed. *What next?* She thought of jumping out of the window, but the rain coming in through the roof caught her attention. There was her hole!

She leaped onto the fallen oak and moved the balls of her feet along its trunk past the crushed wall to get outside. Soft mud splattered beneath her as she fell onto the sodden ground. She tried to breathe amidst her screams and sobs. On shaking legs, she saw the huge tree. During its topple it lifted the ground in which its roots clutched, and crushed a whole corner of the cabin. The roof of the porch was also pressed into the mud under one of the tree's more giant forks. Her sobs came in torrents like the rain that washed drips of blood from her face when she saw her Outback, also crushed under the limbs. How could she get help? A massive and close lightning strike and thunderclap knocked a scream from her throat. The wind roared.

She ran toward the woods, and after only a few steps, the voice that horrified her previously returned. "Beaaaa." Did she hear it again, or was it her terror fooling her? "Beaaa." She was sure she heard it. Why was this place doing this to her?

"Get away!" she screamed. "Get out!" She screamed until her throat burned like fire.

"Beaaa...You shouldn't be here." A cold shiver moved down her spine. It was a voice, she was sure of it now.

"Ahhh!" She screamed toward the voice. "Go Away! Leave me alone!" She ran toward the trees away from the sound and the taloned beast in her cabin. She stumbled in the mud but forced her legs to continue. A cluster of trees caught her panicked attention. They were curved into themselves, making a hollow in which she could hide.

Now hiding in the recess of trees, she focused her eyes on the cabin. There was no movement. She kept her eyes fixed on it, paralyzed with fear. Her chest heaved and jerked from the sprint and the crying.

"Bea!" She heard it again. The direction of the voice was changing. Whoever or whatever it was, it was circling her. "Beaaa!" It continued. She could tell it was coming toward her, so she left her hideaway and ran back toward the cabin, not sure what to do next. What was tormenting her? What did it mean? How did it know her name? As she neared the cabin, she turned back toward the woods and saw nothing but the violent whipping of its trees.

Suddenly, she felt a sting on her head. The owl had returned! Like her, it flew out of the hole in the cabin. She felt the talons digging into her shoulder. She swung her fists but missed him. Ducking the blow, it loosened its grip enough that she could shrug it loose. Where should she go? How could she escape the assault from the crazed owl? She feared nothing more than the cabin. The woods? She feared the woods as well as they were where the voice coming from? Who was it? The winged tormentor flew at her again. Her own voice was now hoarse from screaming. She ran, heaving through sobs.

Falling into the mud, she felt the bird fly over her again. She rose and mustered as much strength as she could and ran for the creek. "My God! Why are you doing this to me?" She screamed with each step. She wanted nothing more of these woods, the cabin, or the world. "Pluck me from it!" she pleaded, each word accompanying a bounding leap. When she reached the creek, she did not slow her sprint. Without hesitation, she leaped into the empty space beyond the overhanging rock of the ravine. With her arms open, she embraced the rocks below.

The following day brought the sun to which the happy valley was accustomed. The rain had exhausted itself, and the clouds thinned and whitened. The songbirds and woodland creatures resumed their symphony. Water in the creek was deep and flowed fast. The large rocks of the creek floor now heaved up heavy pillows of water. The owl was perched upon one of the boulders amidst the churning rainwater and tore small bites of pink flesh from Bea's lifeless shoulder protruding from the water. Her red gown was torn away from the submerged and mangled torso.

After chewing and swallowing a piece of fat, he preened the mottled gray feathers of his chest, making sure every one of them lay properly. The sun reflected from the gloss of its drying feathers as he stretched out his body to absorb the sun. The morning light revealed the intricate patterns of barred lines formed by his overlapped body feathers. Brown feathers the color of wet rust formed a maze pattern and round tufts on his head.

His eyes, different from others of his kind, were not bright nor observant. The expected citrine reflection was not there. The milky eyes neither observed nor accepted the light and were mounted asymmetrically in their sockets. His blindness diminished his otherwise regal pose. He pulled another string of sinewy tissue from his find when a familiar sound caused him to turn his head around its shoulders. The voice from the forest came again, but this time was not muffled by the torrent. The voice was not howling "Beaa" after all, but rather, "Pete."

"Pete!" The owl lengthened his body upward. "Pete! Where are you?" The owl turned toward the voice and leaned into a winding flight out of the ravine. He lifted himself into the air and sailed through the standing trees. "Pete! There you are! Come here, you blind rascal!" Pete the owl circled toward his kind old friend who had been calling his name during the storm. "Pete, I've been worried sick about you. Come on! We don't live here anymore." The owl continued to circle the mass of gray hair and old leather clothes that hobbled toward him. The man underneath them paused and stood straight before resting his legs by squatting on the ground. He whistled and patted the top of his head, which was covered by thick hair and a rabbit-skin hat. Pete recognized the brushy thump-thump-thump of the man's hand on his hat and took the cue to resume his familiar perch. "Dear Lord, Pete! Something could have gotten you. What if those old crows found you?"

Pete dug his claws into the rabbit skin hat, glad to be there. A stiff, leathery hand reached up toward him and the talons released. Pete stepped gingerly onto the hand. The man lowered his friend into his lap and caressed the smooth feathers on Pete's back and shoulders. The old man could no longer withhold the tears that rolled down his nose and into the massive beard beneath it. He had found his blind feathered friend. "I bet you are starving. Let's go. We don't want to bother these nice folks." He lifted Pete and returned him to the top of his head. "Hang on." Pete gripped firmly. The man stood, steadied himself, and sauntered back into the woods, saying, "Looks like old tree finally fell."

Chapter 7

Commedia Dell'arte

The town of Yvoire, France, wakes early in the morning. It always has. The township grew from a medieval fort established on the banks of Lake Geneva. The air is always brisk as it blows around the frozen peaks to its north. Our story took place in 1762, and at that time, it was a bustling trade town that served clay-fired foods to tradesmen, crepes being a favorite. Among its collection of odd characters was Milun Babineaux.

A young man of twenty, Milun swept streets and cleaned the floors of creperies and florists for coins they threw his way. This was not the profession he chose, and he often dreamed of other distinctions not available to him. He was of moderate height with sandy brown hair. He was strong but thin. He walked with a limp and typically wore hats that covered his brow, hiding a scar that extended across his forehead and into his left eyebrow – a feature that made him recognizable but somewhat clownish. Those that recognized him mocked him and pointed him out to others. "There is the boy who was caught spying through windows." This constant threat of humiliation, combined with his awkwardness, forced him to become a man of the shadows.

As a younger man in his late teens, he discovered a pastime. In the evenings, he enjoyed peeping into windows. At the time, he considered it harmless. He found inspiration and enjoyment looking in on families as they dined. He admired their artwork and ornaments on their tables. He was enthralled by the beautiful young maidens and wives as they ate and prepared for bed. This infatuation soon led to watching them as they slept and bathed. More than once, he had caught a glimpse of glistening wet skin made amber from candlelight. Their soapy bosoms and curvy buttocks made his heart race. Until he was discovered.

One particular evening he watched through the window as a young maiden removed her gossamer gown and prepared for the tub. A maid was helping the young lady and noticed the young peeping tom's forehead. In a panic, she hurled an earthenware chamber pot through the window that smashed squarely into Milun's brow, knocking him unconscious. Raising the alarm, men of the house hurried out and saw the young man unconscious at the base of the wall under the window. For good measure, they administered a beating upon his back and limbs as well stomps upon his ribs and gut. One of the large booted feet broke his hip. Upon calling the guard, they identified him as a laborer's son, but because of his age, he was not flogged or jailed. His hip healed.

However, he was left with a lasting limp, and the gash upon his brow formed a scar which would identify him henceforth as the boy who peaked in windows.

Years had passed since that episode, yet he was reminded of it daily. Although fewer and fewer people of the town remembered the event, those that did, whispered, "that boy with the low hat, look at him. He hides a scar from being caught as a prowler and peeping tom."

Milun frequently dreamed of the day when he could leave Yvoire and begrudged the many reasons he could not do so. The main reason was that he had no money. In another town, he would be a beggar and destitute. Despite his humiliation of being recognized and the cruel entertainment others enjoyed at his expense, he survived by sweeping pavements and tossing slop pots for the shopkeepers.

Peeping into windows at bathing women no longer interested him. His daily shame reminded him of its consequences. It was enough to see beautiful ladies walking down the cobblestone streets purchasing their wares and pastries from the shops. He admired their beauty, wishing more than anything he could court one of them, yet it was impossible. He was painfully envious of the young suitors who extended their hand to help them across streets and into carriages. He felt no different than them other than they had family wealth and birthrights, and he was a laborer's son. He observed men from foreign places visiting this town on the edge of Lake Geneva. They were genteel and had proper manners, manners not complex or difficult to mimic. He could move about and gesture in the same graceful and elegant ways they did if he were one of them. If he was a foreigner in their town, he could be exotic and eloquent just as they were. The shopkeepers likewise had no great skill that he could not duplicate. The butchers owned their stores and obtained their means by cutting carcasses into purchasable shapes. Bakers simply kneaded dough and baked wads of them in clay ovens. This was not difficult. He had observed them doing this countless times as he swept the floors for the pittance they tossed him. If only this were him, he thought, in a different town or a different country. It was simply the clothes and mannerisms that made them different. His mother had died when he was still toddling around their simple shack. His father was twenty years older than his mother and worked as a carpenter's assistant. Money was toiled for, and there was little of it left after the rent was paid and a few joints of meat bought for the kettle.

Milun was more at ease during the winter when he wore coats and scarves and hats that would hide his scar and his face. Dressed in thick winter clothing, he could walk and mingle among the townspeople unrecognized, hiding his limp by elongating his gait and moving more gracefully. He had no money to spend at the bakeries or bookshops. He could only walk about the town pretending to have peerage with those who did. Thus, he longed for the day when he could leave Yvoire to start a new and better life in a new town.

One fall morning, Milun was up early after a sleepless night to work at a wine seller who awarded him the honor of washing grime from the gutter between the shop and the street. The morning consisted of pushing the foul grime of the gutter into the larger ditches which ran into the rivers. Hoping to see the metallic glint of a dropped coin, he watched the filth as it sloshed. His attention to the grunge was interrupted as he began noticing the murmurs of the passersby. They were talking about an event that had taken place – something malevolent that jolted them. He moved closer to the street so that he might overhear their words. They were of horror and shock. Someone had been killed. Straining to hear more details of the incident, he continued his sweeping and scrubbing as more townsfolk walked past. As the morning progressed, their murmurs were no longer hushed. Instead, they were talking openly about a tragedy. Some of them pointed toward the alleyway that led to a row of houses belonging to merchants and bankers.

Milun sat his broom aside, donned his low-brimmed hat, and casually walked down the alleyway. At the end, where it opened up on the street, he saw more people gathering around a particular house. They were talking to one another with faces aghast. A guard was there gesturing. Milun moved closer.

To the town's horror, a banker had been murdered in his sleep, his throat slashed. He had no children, but his butler discovered him that morning. Apparently, little was disturbed in the house. Only a floorboard had been torn up, and a lockable box had been destroyed. The lock was busted, and its contents were removed. The banker was known to be a wealthy man, and most figured his little box hid items of value. No one knew for sure, but they guessed the murderer found his motive in the gold coins the box contained. Milun did not tarry long after hearing the news. He did not want his scarred brow to be recognized, and himself be humiliated by comparisons to the murdering type. The guards had no leads on who might have done this, and in the days to come, no further clues presented themselves. Eventually, the events of that morning and the gruesome discovery faded from the daily conversation of the town's inhabitants.

A few weeks later, Milun, this time finding a chore sweeping under the tables of an innkeeper's outdoor eatery, was working to earn a few coins. A group of foreigners came out of the Inn and were chatting over bowls of brothy stew. He did not understand their language as they spoke gaily and with grand gestures. He guessed they were Italians. They wore odd colorful clothes, even for Italians. He continued his sweeping without bothering them, only briefly observing them secretly. They were tall and elegant. The women wore their dark hair down, and the men were finely groomed yet did not bear the ere of aristocracy.

When they finished their bowls, one of the men passed a few coins to the innkeeper that he might place a poster on the wall. The man tacked it up on the wall, and the group moved on down the cobbled street laughing and pointing at the interesting shops of the town. They were actors. The poster read:

Commedia Dell'arte

Two Lovers and a Hound

A play in three parts
On the terrace behind the Inn.

Milun admired their station. This odd bunch, with their olive skin and dark hair, traveled from city to city, country to country, putting on their performances[10]. They would receive applause, warm meals, and soft beds for merely reciting their lines and pantomiming comedic actions. He watched them as they walked out of sight and around the corner through the streets of Yvoire.

Milun finished his sweeping and stepped into the Inn to ask the keeper for his pay. Calling his name, he received no

---

[10] Commedia Dell'arte was a form of European play production popularized in Italy. It featured spoofish renditions of popular mainstream pieces. Performances commonly featured music and pantomime which took liberties with the original plots. Improvisations and bawdy costumes including grotesque masks were common.

reply. The innkeeper was out, and the rooms were deserted. Out of curiosity, he stepped up the stairs to the second floor to the cheaper rooms the players had rented. They likewise were empty. He noticed one of the bedroom doors had not been properly closed, and pressing it with his fingertips, the opening widened. The bed was unmade, and general clutter was scattered about. In the room was a chest that belonged to one of the performers. It was colorful, with Italian words scratched into its enamel paint. Milun walked over to it. It was likewise unlocked, so he lifted the lid. He immediately saw colorful costumes with lace collars and funny hats with bells on the end. He pushed back the costumes to examine the next layer of contents, exposing three masks. They were made of leather with eye openings, and covered the brow and nose of the wearer, but not the mouth. The nose was long and bird-like, and each one bore a different expression. One seemed happy and jovial. Another angry and brooding. The last was sad and had painted tears pouring from its eye holes. Their cheeks were blushed with rouge and augmented with birds' feathers to make the eyebrows. In a tray next to the masks were a few coins. Unable to deny his temptation, he took some of the coins and put them into his pocket. He put the clothes back over the masks and shut the lid of the chest. He stepped out of the room, closing the door completely on his way out.

Two nights later, the play was to be held. Behind the Inn, a series of painted sheets were hung in a semi-circle, making a backdrop for their performance. A crowd had gathered, and a younger member of the troupe was collecting the entrance fee from curious audience members going in. After most of the interested townspeople had entered, Milun stepped forward and gave the young dark-haired boy some of his stolen coins and went in. A row of torches had been erected near the sheets to illuminate the performers' faces and costumes. Each of them wore leathery masks glossed with varnish like he had seen in the chest. The costumes were adorned with glass beads intended to reflect the flickering firelight, which yielded a fairylike effect. The long beak-like proboscises of their masks added a bizarre extremity to their expression.

The play featured two dimwitted lovers who became enamored with each other. They flee the permissions of their kinfolk in a clumsy escape to marry. The first act closed with a calamitous wedding night. The crowd laughed and mocked the idiotic characters of the play until the second act began. In the second act, the new couple has adopted a hound. As their love deteriorates, they bicker over who will keep the dog. In mockery of Romeo and Juliet, the couple commits simultaneous suicide to escape the other. The hound, played by a short man in a furry suit, is elated by their death and trots off happily as the performance concludes.

The actors performed the play the following night, and the next morning packed their belongings and left. Milun returned to his solicitation of undesirable chores. The performance had given a persistent silliness to the demeanor of those who had seen it, behaving with exaggerated gestures and dimwitted pantomimes during their conversations. Milun appreciated their gaiety as it distracted them from them noticing him. Inevitably, in the days to come, the levity faded and the townspeople of Yvoire returned to their typical selves.

A few days later, the morning chatter was dimmed, again by grim news. Another murder. Similar to the previous one, a wealthy man had been killed in his sleep, and his safebox raided. However, this time, there was a witness. The dead man's terrified wife had seen the killer. She was in another room when a dark cloaked figure entered. She heard a scuffle in the master bedroom and went to see what her husband was fussing about. Before she reached the room, the cloaked figure exited but stopped and looked at her. She was horrified and recounted the slayer standing in the entryway to the bedroom while looking at her. She said he was wearing a mask, and as he stepped into candlelight, she could make out its demonic features. It had slanted devilish eyes and a long beak that would haunt her dreams the rest of her days.

The townspeople immediately suspected the performers from the play. It was the same long-nosed mask of the *Commedia Dell'arte*. They called them vile gypsies and cursed their wandering ways. They had come to town to take their money and single out wealthy victims. They wondered what town they were in now executing their despicable plans. Who would go after them?

The countenance of the town remained grim and vengeful for days, and just when the mood of fear was easing, the masked villain returned. A town magistrate had been killed. As before, the master of the house had been slaughtered. Gold had been taken. The killer had been seen, and a pattern was forming. Instead of leaving the house after he had performed the dastardly deed, he sought out the man's children to terrify them. Sneaking into the room where his two young sons were sleeping, he held a candle in front of his masked face. They described the same demonic look with a long beak. The townsfolk were horrified by the audacity of the marauder, as if he wanted to make his presence known. The murders were becoming frequent, and the killer becoming brazen. The Townguard posted a notice for all to keep careful vigilance, and all were given instructions to alarm their doors and keep a watch for strange foreigners.

Talk of the killings dominated the hearts and souls of the townspeople. It was all they could talk about. Wealthy men felt targeted. Each night another attack was expected. Each morning the people rose to expect the news of another slaying. They plotted against the *Commedia Dell'arte* actors, and some suggested that an appointed group of men should go and find what town they are in and bring them to justice. The most vocal among them shouted, "How can we be safe until the whole lot of them is hanged?"

The fall had progressed into winter. Milun's days of sweeping were shorter as the sun descended sooner. Snow fell upon his shoulders as he walked home in his heavy cloak. He opened the door of his father's house and entered, voicing a few kind words to his aging patriarch. His father was sitting by the fire stirring a boiling pot, exhausted from his day of labor. Milun rested a kind hand upon his shoulder before going upstairs to his loft. His room was lit by a candle as he sat upon his bed. He did not know how much longer he would be in this town, but hoped the days were few. As his father drifted off to sleep, Milun reached under his mattress for the bag of gold coins he had been collecting. His treasure was growing, and in the near future, he would have enough to leave the town of Yvoire and travel to a distant country. He did not yet know what trade he would adopt. Perhaps he would buy a bakery and make the pastries that he had observed being made as he cleaned. Maybe a butcher. A florist. He had watched them all and saw that there was little to it. He had no doubt he could perform the tasks just as he had beheld. His time as a humiliated cleaner of filth had been an apprenticeship as he noted the day-to-day work of the various tradesmen. He went to sleep and dreamt of far-off cities busy with beautiful people visiting his shop, of which he was the master.

Two weeks later, tragedy struck again in the town of Yvoire. This time it was the innkeeper. It was well after midnight when a cloaked figure stepped silently into the entranceway. His face was covered, but it didn't matter, for everyone was asleep, including the innkeeper. The masked man moved soundlessly toward the innkeeper's room. With a blade in hand, he opened the door. Within a few steps, he was standing next to the sleeping innkeeper. He plunged his blade completely through the neck, and with slicing saws upward, his lifeblood sprayed, and air bubbled. The innkeeper opened his eyes for a moment but could not make any sound, and a second later, he was dead. The killer walked over to the armoire, where he knew the gold was kept. The door creaked slightly as he opened it, but now it didn't matter. He took it all. Finished with his task, he walked out of the room and closed the door behind him.

Putting the sack of gold in his cloak, he stepped out of the Inn into the snowy night. He looked up at the moon. Snow fell upon his varnished mask. He began his way back to his lair when a voice shouted at him. "Hey! You there! Halt!" It was a guard. The spree of martyrs had intensified their nighttime vigilance. The guard suspected malfeasance and drew his sword as he walked toward the cloaked figure. The killer had not expected this. He thought about running but knew his limp would slow him. He had no choice but to face the guard. He drew his knife, still soiled by the innkeeper's blood. The guard beheld the bloody knife and the long-beaked mask. He suspected correctly that the killer was back and he had caught him. The guard swung his sword, but the killer muted the blow with the knife. The guard, with fury, swung again, this time knocking the knife from the killer's hand. Now unarmed, the killer had no choice but to run, but the guard had already plunged his sword into the killer's back. The murderer fell and rolled upon the snow. The guard drew back his sword and plunged it into the chest of the villain. The murderer became still as his lifeblood spilled onto the snowy street.

The guard had done his duty. The murdering menace of Yvoire, France, was no more. The greedy motive of the killer had played out. His final act had been performed. Dreams of setting up shop in a foreign town ceased. Milun Babineaux was dead.

Chapter 8

Pocket

A man named August McLaren leaned his bicycle against the old brown stone wall of St. Matthew's Church in North Berwick, Scotland. He was twenty-eight years old, and the intensity of his angst was higher than usual as he knocked on the office door of Father Agravain Eideard for his 3:30pm appointment.

"Hello August," said Father Eideard, "come in."

"Thank you, Father," said August, "thanks for seeing me."

"Not a problem, it's good to see you. How have you been?"

"Okay, I guess. And you Father, how have you been?"

"Oh, just fine. Please sit down, relax. How is your mother?"

"She is holding tight for now, but lately has not been feeling well."

"What's ailing her?"

"She is not sure. For the past few weeks she says she has no energy."

"That's not good."

"No, but I took her to the doctor a couple days ago. They drew some labs, and she is waiting on results. Maybe they will show something."

"Let's hope so."

"Thank you, Father."

"Tell me, August, how is the book coming?"

"Well, you know how it goes – it's going. I've been working on some short stories."

"That sounds fun. Are you having any luck?"

"Oh, a little, I guess."

"Why do you say it like that?" asked Father Eideard, "good luck can't be bad."

"That's what I wanted to see you about."

"Oh?"

"Yes, Father. My luck has been a little atypical lately."

"Ah, the tortured writer, you fit the mold so well. Tortured with good fortune and bad."

"Yes, I guess so."

"So, tell me about this good fortune that has gotten you so bothered."

"I'll do my best, but it's hard to describe and sound believable."

"I'm sure a man of words like yourself will be able to find a way."

"Well, a few weeks ago, there was an advertisement in the back of the Edinburgh Writer's Collective calling for short stories to be submitted for consideration. So, of course, I was excited about the possibility of one being published."

"Good for you August, you must always be looking for an opportunity for an audience to find you."

"Yes Father, well, I had been working on an odd story about a drifting bloke, who was down to his last dime, and was going to jump off of a bridge, when out of the blue, a rich relative passed away and left him a big chunk of money."

"That sounds interesting, a common plot of course, so I'm sure you had a clever ending to make it stand out."

"Well, you see, that's just it. I didn't."

"I see."

"But, I had a few ideas. Late one evening, I was pondering how I might end the story, but became sleepy as I thought of possible endings. So, I folded the partial manuscript and put it into my pocket. The next morning when I got up, I tuned in on the radio, and Jed at the station was giving the local news, and you wouldn't believe it. He said a North Berwick man, down on his luck, just received a fortune from an uncle who had passed."

"Ah, coincidences are something, aren't they?"

"They sure are. And, that's just what I thought. So since the same events as in my story had happened to that fella, I thought it best to shelf the idea since it no longer seemed that original."

"I see."

"Not a big deal. I had a few other stories in reserve. So, I picked a different one from the old mental vault."

"That's a boy."

"The one I went with was about an American girl who falls in love with a foreigner with a mysterious background, but he turns out to be wanted by Interpol for stealing old paintings. I finished the first draft and was planning to start the rewrite the next day. Feeling like this was good, I put the story in my pocket and went to bed. The next day I was out for coffee, and I saw this in The Herald." Father Eideard took the folded newspaper clipping August held out for him. Unfolding it, he read the headline. "Art Thief Discovered in America." He read it as August continued, "you see, Father? In the column? It's an American girl who discovers her lover to be a villain, in just the same way as in my story."

"August, is this what has gotten you so bothered? Those types of coincidences happen all the time. You mustn't think anything of them."

"I agree completely. So to prevent overly common occurrences from coinciding with my short stories, I resolved to write something local and very specific."

"That sounds like good logic – And?"

"I wrote a story about a child from North Berwick who was stolen as a baby, and raised in France. She is smart, and goes to a fancy college and then is hired by a large investment firm, and eventually makes herself a boatload of money. For no reason, other than curiosity, she looks into her ancestry and submits a DNA sample, only to discover who she really is. She meets her original family, and with her own money buys a manor overlooking Milsey Bay. Well then, as you can now guess, I put the unfinished draft in my pocket, and sure enough, the very next day, it was announced that little Davina Donhall was found in France and was coming back to North Berwick, and was buying a manor on the Bay with her own money. Turns out, she had been stolen by a childless family from Devonshire and had been named Deidra Ferris. These things just keep happening."

"I did hear about Davina Donhall being found and returning," said Father Eideard. "I admit that is an amazing coincidence, and I'm sure you're bound to think something is amiss, but it just simply can't be. August, you know in your God-fearing soul this is not possible. It is merely a profound coincidence. You can't get so worked up."

"I tell you, I agree Father, and I put it out of my mind, and just to prove to myself it was impossible, I wrote a funny little limerick and put it in my pocket."

"Let's hear it."

"If true they be, the stories I've told, then on my steps bring coins of gold."

"Ah, good thinking. Are you satisfied then?" August reached into his pocket and took out four gold coins, and laid them on the desk in front of Father Eideard. "Wow, August, where did you get these?"

"I swear on my soul Father, they were on my doorstep the next morning. The same as the words of the limerick in my pocket."

"This is unbelievable."

"I know, I still don't believe it myself."

"So August, how can I help you with this?"

"Maybe you could suggest a few words to write, and maybe that will prove this is impossible."

"August, I'm sure this is not necessary."

"Again Father, I agree, but maybe you could humor me."

"Okay August, let's make it fun." Father Eideard thought for a moment with his fingers flicking the mustache that covered his lips and rubbing his bald head until a clever idea formed. "Okay, I have two for you." August retrieved a pen and tablet of paper from his shirt pocket. "First, a local church, St. Matthew's of course, receives half-million pound donation to build a park in town." August scribbled a few sentences on the memo pad, tore off the sheet, and put it into his pocket. "And the second one; your mother finds out what has gotten her down lately, and it is resolved by the doctors so that her energy returns and she is able to attend services."

"Very good Father." August scribbled the words and likewise put the paper into his pocket. "So, I'll see you in the morning then?"

"If you need to August, though I think this will put it to bed."

"Okay, Father, and thank you very much."

"It's been my pleasure, and keep visiting. It's really good to hear you are staying diligent with your writing. I'm certain you will catch a break soon."

August mounted his bicycle and pedaled home. Walking into his house, he greeted his mother who was sitting at the table. Her face was pale and her hands trembled as she sipped her tea. "Hello Mum, how are you feeling today?"

"Just tired as usual."

"You want me to make you breakfast?"

"No, I can manage. I made some toast." August walked past the kitchen, its yellow curtains created a warmly lighted space filled with the smell of toasting bread. Three months ago, his mother would have been making a pie and singing as she moved about the home she had decorated so carefully. Now, she was just too exhausted.

In his room, he picked up the April edition of the Edinburgh Writer's Collective. He read one of the short stories by an American from New York. *This story is no different than anyone else's who submitted a manuscript,* he thought. *What political pull does this bloke have that got him published? Who are the aloof and insular editors that choose these and reject others? They know nothing.* He spent the day writing the stories in his mind and reading those of others, keeping the notes dictated by Father Eideard in his pocket until bedtime.

In the morning, he woke and started his usual routine with a cup of coffee. Sitting at the round table in his mother's yellow-curtained kitchen, he closed his eyes and inhaled the enlivening aroma of the "elixir of roasted beans" when the phone rang. "Hello?" He said.

"Yes, this is Mazie at Dr. Raith's office, is Mrs. Vivian McLaren available?"

"I am her son, can I help you?"

"We got her thyroid results back, and her levels are low. Dr. Raith says this is likely why she has been feeling tired. He would like to see her soon and has prescribed her some supplemental thyroid hormone."

"Oh, that's great! I can bring her most any time, and I will pick up the meds for her right away."

"Can you bring her by tomorrow?"

"Yes, what time?"

"How about 11:00am?"

"Perfect, see you then." After hanging up, August phoned the pharmacy to have the meds delivered to the house right away.

"Who was that?" asked his mother Vivian as she slowly walked into the kitchen.

"Mum! It was Dr. Raith's office. The nurse says your thyroid is low."

"Really?"

"Yes, I called the pharmacy to have the meds he prescribed delivered here. He wants to see you tomorrow. Doc thinks that is why you have felt so tired."

"Oh, good."

"You bet it is." He stood and tucked his shirt into his pants and put on his shoes.

"Where are you headed?"

"I'm gonna go out for a stroll." He kissed his mother on the cheek, stepped outside, and mounted his bicycle. Peddling straight to St. Matthew's, he knocked on Father Eideard's office door.

Father Eideard answered the door and said, "You better come in and sit down." August walked in and sat in one of the high-backed office chairs with sky-blue burlap upholstery. "August you won't believe what the carrier delivered about an hour ago."

"What is it Father?"

"You know Widow Gillean?"

"Yes."

"Well, she died apparently."

"Oh, that's too bad."

"Her niece wrote me to say that in her will, she left half a million to the church with the request that it go toward constructing a park."

"Holy smokes! Well you aren't going to believe the call I got from Dr. Raith's office this morning either." Father

Eideard's face was stern and flushed. "The nurse called to say that Mum's thyroid was low, and that's why she feels bad."

"You don't say!"

"Yes, Father, I tell you this defies all logic."

"Now hold on August. I know this seems unbelievable, but it's impossible to be anything than just an uncanny coincidence."

"Shall we have another try, just to make sure?"

"Yes my boy, we should. Let's put this craziness to rest right away." August picked up the writing pad from the table near the blue chair. He sat pencil-in-hand, waiting for a suggestion from Father Eideard. "It needs to be an event that would confound all doubt if it comes to pass. What shall it be... Aha! I have it. Down in the basement of the church is an old locked closet. There is nothing in it but old mops and buckets, however the lock is one hundred and fifty years old and it seems a shame to break it. But the key was lost about twenty years ago. Get your pencil August, write this down. 'The key to the mop closet downstairs in St. Matthew's Church, shall be delivered to Father Eideard.'"

"Oh, that's a good one Father."

"Furthermore, when the stranger delivers it, he shall recite to me unprompted the Burns poem, 'My Heart is in the Highlands.'"

"Indeed! And, also, the stranger shall give me a car," added August.

"Good thinking. Now write it down on your papers. If *these* things come to pass, there will be no doubt something strange but certain is among us. Tomorrow will bring closure to the coincidences."

"Aye, so it will." With that, August McLaren mounted his bicycle and pedaled back to his mother, but in his pocket was a piece of paper with penciled words saying:

"A stranger to Father Eideard brought him the lost key to the downstairs mop closet and recited, 'My Home is in the Highlands.' Then the stranger gave me a car."

When August arrived home, his spirits were high. He made himself a pot of tea and worked into the night on a novel whose pages he had forsaken for quite some time, but made sure the slip of paper was in his pocket when he went to bed. The next morning he slept later than usual, but arising at 9:00am he prepared to take his mother to Dr. Raith's office. Their neighbor, Mrs. Dunsmore, allowed him to use her car anytime he needed to take Vivian to the doctor. That was his plan this morning. He was putting on his shoes to make sure it was okay with Mrs. Dunsmore that he use the car, when a knock came at the door. August answered it. "Uncle Baird?"

"How are you lad?" asked Uncle Baird.

"I'm great. How have you been?"

"Not too bad, not too bad. I'm glad I caught you. I've got a proposition for you."

"Oh, okay, well come in. Please sit down. Care for some coffee?"

"No, lad, I've had a peck already. How is your mother?"

"She's a little tired lately. We are headed to the doctor's here shortly."

"Is that so?"

"Yes, they say her thyroid is low."

"That must be why she feels so tired," said Uncle Baird. "She sounded weak the last few times I phoned her. It's got me worried. Now her little brother gets to worry about her. Which is why I'm here. I'm getting a new car."

"A new car?"

"Yes."

"That's great. What kind?"

"I'm on my way downtown to pick up a new Audi A4."

"Wow, that's nice Uncle Baird."

"Thanks lad. I have my old Vauxhall Zafire to trade-in, but they ain't gonna give me much of nothing for it. So if you'll take it, I'll give it to you for taking my sister to the doctor."

"Wow, Uncle Baird, that is very thoughtful of you. Thank you very much."

"Say nothing of it. When is her next appointment?"

"Well, it's in two hours."

"Superb! Here you go," said Uncle Baird, handing August the keys. "It leaks a little oil, and pulls to the left, but all in all she is still a good one."

"Is that Baird I here?" said Vivian coming into the kitchen.

"Hey, Sis," said Uncle Baird. "You still getting around?"

"Oh, I guess so. I'm just so tired."

"August tells me the doc thinks it may be your thyroid."

"Yes, that's what he says," she said.

"Well, maybe they can get you back at full speed."

"I think it will," said August. "Mother, you should know, Uncle Baird just gave us his Vauxhall."

"Why did you do that Baird?

"I'm getting a new A4 today. In fact, I was hoping I could ride into town with you. On your way to the doctor you can drop me off at the Audi dealer."

"Baird, of course we are happy to take you, but you can't give us your car."

"Oh, Sis, you don't worry about that. It ain't worth much, and August takes good care of you."

"That he does Baird, that he does."

"Well, anyhow, thanks-a-million Uncle Baird," said August.

"Why certainly, you are welcome."

August drove Baird and Vivian into town with the Vauxhall. He dropped Baird at the Audi dealer and thanked him profusely. "I hope you like the new one," said August. "Will you bring it by the house?"

"You bet, lad. I have a few stops to make first. Viv, I hope the doctor has good news."

"I'm sure he will. Thanks again Baird."

Once at Dr. Raith's, August sat next to his mother while waiting on the nurse to come get them and show them to the exam room. He thought about the car and the written words he put into his pocket last night. There can be no doubt now, there *was* something happening. *Wait until Father Eideard hears about this,* he thought.

Meanwhile, Uncle Baird had gotten his new Audi and was driving it around North Berwick. He stopped and got some coffee and sipped it while listening to Jethro Tull through his high-definition car speakers. His next stop was St. Matthew's. He pulled into the lot, then walked to the side door of the auditorium. It had been twenty years since he had been inside, and the high vaulted ceilings and stained glass windows still struck him with awe.

"Can I help you?" asked a voice. Uncle Baird turned to see Father Eideard walking toward him.

"Hello, my name is Baird Sinclair. I used to attend here, years ago. My sister and nephew still do. I'm sure you know Vivian McLaren and her son August." Father Eideard felt his heart skip a beat when the stranger mentioned August's name. The words written the day before were supposed to disprove unnatural coincidences, but yet here was a stranger. Baird reached into his pocket and produced an old skeleton key.

"What is this Mr. Sinclair?"

"I found this the other day. Before I moved off to university, I used to help out with maintenance on the grounds to earn a few extra quid. Well, I must have had this old key on my person on my last day. I would have brought it back sooner, but you know how it goes, I forgot all about it. I've had it in my sock drawer for twenty years. It goes to an old closet downstairs, I'm sure you know the one. I happened to remember it on my way to North Berwick this morning."

"How remarkable. Yes, I know the door. It is still locked. Thank you." Father Eideard turned pale. He could not believe what he was hearing. Trying to regain his composure, he forced himself to converse normally with Baird. "Well, Mr. Sinclair, what have you been up to lately?"

"Oh, not much Father. My work keeps me busy. I've been traveling some, and I perform in community theater on Thursdays."

"Really? What sort of plays?"

"Oh, silly little things for tourists. I've been portraying the old Bard." Baird placed his hand over his heart and assumed the character he had been practicing. He recited,

"*Farewell to the Highlands, farewell to the North,*
the birthplace of valor, the country of worth;
wherever I wonder, wherever I rove,
the hills of the Highlands, forever I love."

Father Eideard nearly fainted. He swallowed hard in disbelief and said, "That's great Mr. Sinclair, and it is wonderful to meet you."

"Likewise, Father, I'll be on my way, and you have a wonderful day." *What a strange character,* thought Baird.

After his visitor left, Father Eideard sat down in one of the pews. A thousand thoughts flooded into his mind. All doubt was gone. Baird's visit proved it. It was certain. He wondered, Why *August? Why is this ability wasted on a lout like him? He could save the world if he wasn't such a buffoon.* Father Eideard sat in silent amazement staring at the vaulted ceilings.

August was taking it well, knowing whatever was written and put into his pocket when he went to sleep would come true the next day. Life was looking good for him. Getting Baird's Vauxhall solved the issue of transportation. He wrote that there would appear fifty thousand in cash in a shoebox on his doorstep - it came true. That night he took himself to a restaurant in North Berwick, and ordered lobster and a bottle of red wine. He sat at the bar after the meal. A man next to him said, "Looks like things are going good for you young fella."

"Indeed, they are," said August. Something unnerved him about the man who spoke to him with his red grimy hair pulled back into a ponytail and his face unshaved. That strangers might be curious about him made him think as he drove the Vauxhall home. *I can't be throwing around cash. I can't attract attention. How long will I have this ability? What if someone finds out? I'll secure a bit of cash so I can take care of Mum, and maybe get a publishing deal, but I'll remain modest and tell no one. Only Father Eideard will know, and he can help me with philanthropy.*

For the next two days he worked on his novel. With the recent turn of events lifting his spirits, his mind was ablaze with ideas to pen. On a Friday morning, he woke up and fixed himself a breakfast. Vivian was also up in the kitchen preparing to go to the grocery to get the makings for Sunday lunch. She was already feeling better since starting the thyroid meds.

"What are you up to this morning, August?" she asked.

"I'm going to go for a walk, then work on my novel."

"Are you making good progress?"

"Yes, I think one of my short stories is going to appear in the next issue of the Edinburgh Writer's Collective."

"That's wonderful Son. Your hard work is paying off."

"Thanks Mum. It's good to see you smiling. You look like you feel better."

"Oh yes. I feel much better. In fact, I might drive the Vauxhall to the grocery myself."

"That sounds good. Keys are in the drawer."

"Well then, that's what I'll do. Now you go on your walk, and don't worry about me."

It was a summer morning, and the colors were vivid as August walked briskly down the sidewalk. It was two miles to the library in town. It was one of his favorite places to go with its dandelion-colored reading room. Tan two-story houses with red clay shingles on his left and a golf course and the saltwater of the sea on his right lined his way during his walk. The old library was full of leather-bound classics, and grouchy librarians to watch over them.

"Hello Mr. McLaren, how is the novel coming?" asked old Ms. Elsie Dempster, the matron and head of the library.

"It's coming along Ms. Dempster. Thanks for asking."

"Any luck with publications?"

"Well, perhaps. I expect to have a short story in the Collective's next issue."

"That's a fine start my boy, a fine start."

"Thanks." He ran his fingers over the smooth leather spines of the great works, and wondered if old dusty libraries like this one would contain books of his after he was dead. Finished with his daydreaming he began his walk back.

The green horizon of the course fairways cut a contrasting line into the salty water of Milsey Bay with its large ship-sized boulder awkwardly impeding the waters of the Bay. Looking at the breaking crests of the waves, a black Nissan pulled up next to him. There were two men inside. *Probably lost out-of-towners looking for directions.* The car stopped next to him. Instead of rolling down the window, the driver got out, and walked toward him. He was wearing dark sunglasses and a medical grade mask over his mouth and nose.

He wore a blue cap pulled down over his brow so little of his face could be seen.

"Hello my friend. We are looking for August McLaren." After saying this, the other man, who was in the backseat, also climbed out of the car. The second man was similarly attired with sunglasses and a mask to hide his face.

"What do you need with August McLaren?"

"We need him to get in the car with us." August turned to run but he didn't get far before the man from the backseat grabbed him and held him until the driver could grab his other arm. The two of them dragged August and threw him into the backseat. They did all this in a matter of seconds. The driver resumed his seat behind the wheel, now with two passengers in the back. "Now August, there is no need to make this a stressful situation," said the driver. His accent was Scottish, but not from North Berwick. "We understand you have taken something that doesn't belong to you, and the owner wants it back."

"That's absurd! I've taken nothing from no one."

"Now August, don't get so worked up! We are taking you to a place where this can all be resolved." The thug in the backseat with him continued to remain silent but produced a black fabric hood and was proceeding to put it over August's head.

August fought and shouted, "no I can't leave my mother…" The backseat thug punched August hard in the ribs, knocking the wind from him. He put the hood over his head, and zip-tied his wrists.

They drove the car for what seemed like two hours, around curves and cobblestone roads that made August lose his bearings. He no longer knew where he was. When they finally stopped, the two men got him out of the car and led him down four steps that were sandy under his feet. He felt the space become cool around him as if he were in a basement or underground room.

"So long friend," said the driver snidely. August heard the footsteps of the two men leave in the direction from which they had brought him and shut a metal door.

"Hello August," said a new voice. "Let's get that hood off of you." When the hood was taken off, he felt the cool air of the subterranean space fill his lungs. The room he was in looked like it was used for storage and recently cleaned out, painted, and sparsely furnished. The floor was concrete, and bore the appearance of having been just mopped, and smelled of Pine-Sol. In the middle of the floor was a round red and orange woven rug, atop which was a card table and two wooden chairs. Above the table hung a light with a new off-white globe, with a sticker still adhered to the side. A twin bed with a green army blanket sat against the wall, freshly painted white, opposite the door. The room had a commode in the corner, like a prison cell. There was no toilet paper, but rather a bidet attachment on the bowl.

The man who removed the hood, and was now cutting the ties on August's wrists, wore a clown mask over his face. He was a large man and appeared strong, but had a few wisps of a gray beard poking out of the edges of the mask. "August, I owe you an explanation. I'm sure all of this must seem very strange to you. I'm aware that you have a gift, and I know you are aware this *gift* is very powerful."

"I have no gift! What are you talking about? Those thugs said I had taken something. I have not taken anything."

"I know August, I know. I told them you had stolen some money, just to give them a reason for why I sent them after you. I know you have not taken anything. Don't worry about them. You'll never see them again. In fact, they are both out on bail for petty theft and will both receive a few years for their foolishness when they see the judge."

"What do you want from me?"

"It's simple August. I need for you to make a few things happen."

"Why me?"

"Don't be silly August. You have a gift, and you know it."

"Why do you say that?"

"Don't play dumb. It annoys me. Please sit down."

"Tell me what you want first."

"I want you to sit down."

"I don't want to." The man in the clown mask drew back and punched August, hard, in the face, knocking him down. The big meaty hand, with whiskery knuckles, bloodied August's lip.

"I told you August, I get annoyed," the voice behind the clown mask said calmly. August got up from the floor and sat in one of the chairs. In addition to blood coming from his mouth, he had tears coming from his eyes. The man in the clown mask sat in the other chair across from him. "There is no need to make this difficult. I just need you to write a few things down for me."

"How did you find out? Who told you?"

"No one told me. I'm a very observant fellow. I've been watching you."

"I don't want to help you." The man slapped August with the back of his hand, knocking him out of the chair. His face stung, and his voice trembled as he cried. "How long will you keep me here?"

"Not long, I promise you. I just need you to write a few things for me, and after a sufficient time, I will release you, and that is my promise. When I promise something, you can count on it. If you don't cooperate or write the things I ask you, I will have to hurt you more, that is also a promise." From the man's shirt pocket he produced a memo pad and a dull pencil. "Now August, let's start out easy. We need to make sure this works. We need a little working capital. Please write, 'ten thousand quid appear in a brown bag, under the oak tree outside.'"

August wrote the sentence verbatim on the pad. The man tore off the note, "now put it in your pocket, and that will be it for today." He did as he was told. "Thank you." The man stood up and left the room, locking the metal door behind him. A few minutes later, he returned with a sandwich wrapped in foil, and a thermos of tea. He placed the pad of paper, and the pencil, back in his pocket. He walked over to August and patted him on the back, then frisked him. He took his wallet and checked his pockets to make sure there was nothing in them. "Now, just relax. I'll see you in the morning." August said nothing as the man left the room. He paced the empty room with fits of anxiety for hours before eventually lying on the bed, but found it difficult to sleep. The hours ticked by slowly and he was not sure what time it was. But he eventually dozed off with tears drying on his face.

The next morning the man was back and still wearing the clown mask. "Well August, you are truly a man of miraculous ability." He set a paper bag on the card table, and took out of a bundle of British pounds. "Remarkable."

"I need to go. My mother is old and sick. I need to be with her."

"I understand. You are a good son." The man pulled the memo pad out of his shirt pocket. "Why don't you write her a note, and I'll see to it that she gets it. Let her know you are doing well. Tell her you decided to go on a little trip and will be back soon. August, don't worry. You *will* be back soon." August wrote a note to his mother as the man directed.

After putting the note to Vivian in his pocket, the man set a box of pastries on the table for August's breakfast, along with the thermos, now filled with coffee. "Eat well my boy, keep your spirits up. Now, I need you to write another note for me. 'The man in the blue house that hits his mother is run over by a truck on his way to work.'" August looked at him, the man of paradox. The very man who held him prisoner, and slapped and punched him while using calm and kind words, now seemed to be looking out for some abused elder. The act was benevolent in a way, yet his bruised face and swollen lip reminded him of the violence that was *promised* if he did not comply. He wrote the words in compliance. "Now August, let's do a little something for you. Please write, 'when released from here, your next book will sell over a million copies.' See lad, I'm on your side. Now, spend the day in peace and dream of your future success in the coming weeks."

"Weeks? Will I be here for weeks?"

"Roughly. I have a few things I need your help with." August tried his best to sit calmly, yet tears came to his eyes.

The next day was the same. "August, a crying and hurting widow much appreciates the kindness this day has brought her. And, though she doesn't know it, it's thanks to you."

"What will it be today?"

"That's the spirit! Today's requests are a little different. Please write, 'The lot with the old crumbling Inn will be condemned and zoned commercial.' I know this seems a bit trivial, but I assure you it will do much good." August was given the memo pad, and he wrote the words as ordered.

"May I have some writing materials in order to work on my own things while I'm kept here?"

"I understand the request, but alas, I cannot allow it. You might write down that you wish me to be struck by lightning. That would not be in *my* best interest. Another note I would like you to write is that the two men who brought you here, smashed into the bridge on the drive to their flat, and do not survive."

"That's murder!"

The man smirked. "No August, oh no, it will be an accident." August wrote it as demanded. "Thanks, you are doing great. I'll see you in the morning."

When morning came, the man arrived with August's breakfast. "You are doing great! Your 'gift' is proving to be very productive. I have brought you a few things to eat and enjoy. I will be gone until tomorrow. The man unwrapped two sandwiches from their foil, and a hot shepherd's pie in a crock. "Enjoy!"

That evening, Father Eideard had a secret meeting at the house of the man who had been his lover for more than a decade. The two of them hid their relationship and had never been seen in public together.

"I regret telling you. This will not turn out good," said Father Eideard.

"Calm yourself Agravain. I told you, it will be fine. I made you a promise."

"You and your promises. We can't let anything happen to him. How will you be sure he won't recognize you?"

"I've been wearing the clown mask."

"Good God! Poor August, you've probably scared him senseless."

"He seems to be calming. I had him write a note to his mother."

"I must go see Vivian. She is probably worried sick. I need to make sure she doesn't call the police. August is not the type who goes on sudden trips. Oliver, we can't hurt him, and if he sees your face, the plan will be foiled. Furthermore, all he has to do is write on the paper that you fall over dead, and that's it! This is too dangerous. Call it off! Let him go!"

"This is not my first adventure, Agravain. He won't see my face. And the room is completely empty of paper or anything to write with unless I give it to him."

"Well just hurry! Get him to write what we need, then let him go. I don't want any more blood on my hands."

"Relax Agravain, all these sons of bitches who will meet their end are pariahs to the world," said Oliver.

"I know, but make it short."

"Agreed. What should I have him write next?"

"We could use a little more cash. And, that molesting bastard from Dirleton should be dealt with."

"I'll see to it."

"Make sure August is well taken care of."

"I made sure he wrote himself a little 'literary success.'"

"Fine. I need to get back."

"Drive safe. I will talk to August in the morning."

"Don't hurt him!"

"Stop worrying!"

Oliver donned the clown mask before opening the door. "Good morning August." August said nothing. "I hope you are sleeping well?"

"How much longer are you going to keep me?"

"Not much longer, my boy. Don't you worry."

"Are you going to kill me?"

"No, and that I promise you, and you know if I promise anything..."

"Yeah yeah yeah. I know. You keep your promises. So you said. What do you want of me today?"

Oliver sat at the table across from August, who was already sitting. He placed a pad of paper in front of him, and handed him the pencil. "First, I need another sack of cash under the oak tree."

August wrote, "another sack with ten thousand pounds appears under the oak tree." He tore off the sheet of paper and handed it to Oliver who confirmed the words.

"Good. Next, 'the old molester from Dirleton jumps off of a bridge and drowns.'" August began writing the words, but pressed the pencil lead to the paper causing the graphite point to break.

"Dammit," said August. "Can you sharpen this, please?" Oliver pulled out a small bone-handled pocketknife and whittled a new point onto the pencil before handing it back to August. Oliver then examined the words on the second note.

"Now into this magical pocket of yours." August did as he was told and put the slip of paper into his pocket. Then, Oliver left the room, taking the pad of paper and pencil with him.

After he left, August felt around on the rug beneath the table for the graphite splinter he broke off of the pencil. He found it. Though the tiny piece of pencil lead was smaller than a grain of rice, he removed the pieces of paper from his pocket and on the blank side of one of them, made words by pressing the graphite shard onto the paper with his fingertip. He wrote: "the oak tree falls and crushes my prison. My captors are killed."

His mind raced with the thoughts of how and when the words he had written would work. He had no doubts that the words would be fulfilled as strangely as the others had.

Though he had no clock, he felt as if he had lain sleeplessly in his bed until after midnight. Suddenly, he sat up. He knew he needed to add to the collection of sentences expected to come true in the morning. August used the remaining fragment of the pencil lead to mark upon the paper in his pocket. He wrote, "the gift is no more." After writing these words, his mind was instantly at ease. He had pulled off a checkmate against his captors. He laid back onto the thin pillow of the bed and waited with satisfaction.

He was awakened by a sudden rumbling crash. One of the walls of his room had just pulled away from the top edge of the ceiling. August knew instantly, before even seeing it, that an oak tree outside had fallen and crushed part of the wall. Using one of the chairs from the card table, he climbed out of the gap between the wall and the ceiling and into the morning sun. Once on the ground, he knew where he was; just on the edge of North Berwick. The two goons had not driven him out of town after all, just around in circles to the edge of town.

As he walked back to his house, he hoped his mother was doing okay, and he pondered what he would tell her to explain his absence. He would apologize for the sudden impulse of leaving, but would avoid upsetting her by attempting to tell the unbelievable truth. Though the experience of the last few days had been horrific, his anxiety was rapidly resolving. He remembered the words he had written and placed in his pocket that destroyed his confinement and his captor. He wondered if he would ever know who it was behind the mask. He was also glad the gift was gone, and his future excited him.

Two weeks later, he sat at the desk in his room, while his mother, who was feeling much better, was back to her regular self, singing with the songs that played on the radio. August was working on the climax of his latest novel, about a man who had the strangest experience. The main character had a "gift," in the form of an ability to cause things to happen by writing them and putting it in his pocket. He had no doubt it would be published, and even a screenplay be accepted after his recent good luck of having several short stories published. The success of his short stories had prompted publishers to call him with desires to print any manuscripts he had.

Next to him was a newspaper. On the second page was an article about Father Eideard, who along with a companion, had been struck by lightning during a rendezvous in the neighboring town. The article included a picture of both of them, the one of Father Eideard was a few years old, and the one of his companion was the same gray-haired man behind the clown mask. His name was Oliver Brown, and was a retired Army Sergeant. His shoulders slumped in the unmistakable profile of the fiend who talked calmly as he slapped and punched him into submission.

"You vile sons of bitches," said August.

Chapter 9

The Gray Buffalo

When I was a kid, I got to meet Iron Eyes Cody, the famous Native American actor. It was during a Cub Scout den meeting in which we gathered at a native American Pow Wow being held at a nearby state park. These Pow Wows and cultural heritage gatherings only occurred every few years, and the den leaders knew it would be an excellent time to explore the historical cultures of our region. When we arrived at the Pow Wow, we were immediately amazed by the colors and enormity of it all. There were authentic Teepees, which were much bigger in person than we thought they would be. There were circles of men singing loud songs as they beat fast rhythms on huge drums made of skins. As small Cub Scouts, we were astounded and a little intimidated.

We did not get too close, but we watched with amazement. At the time, Iron Eyes Cody[11] was in town filming a movie called *Ernest Goes to Camp.* The filming was happening at the same park at which the Pow Wow was held. He was a friendly person and was very approachable, though he didn't say much. He was quite tall and thin and wore a long shirt made of deerskin. His pants were also deerskin and revealed a pair of decorated moccasins on his feet. A row of beaded cloth was draped over his shoulders on both sides.

The blue and yellow uniforms we wore caught his attention. He walked over to us, and the den of boys slowly gathered around him. To us, he appeared ancient as he stood with a sun-weathered face and feathers in his graying braids. He looked at us with his flinty eyes and gave us a faint smile. "Hello," he said. "Do you have any questions?" No one said anything. I don't know why, but he turned toward me and asked, "What about you, young man?" For a moment, I froze and didn't know what to say. My brain frantically sorted through the millions of questions I could ask. Being suddenly put on the spot I searched my young mind for an appropriate question. Finally, I was able to ask a stuttering question about buffaloes. I am not entirely sure why I chose this question. I

---

[11] Iron Eyes Cody was an Italian American actor who portrayed Native Americans in movies and television commercials. He so immersed himself in the Native American culture that he lived daily as if he were culturally an Indentions American, denied his Italian heritage, and at the time, was largely embraced by many Native American tribes. Despite his controversial heritage, he was an effective advocate for Native American rights and environmental responsibility.

had never seen a buffalo in real life. I had seen many deer on the farm where I grew up, but I had never seen a buffalo.

"Have you ever been buffalo hunting?" I asked.

Iron Eyes Cody shook his head slowly. "No, I have never hunted the buffalo, but my grandfathers did." There was silence for a moment. "Have you seen a buffalo?" He asked.

"No, I never have," I said.

"This is a rare chance for a young man to ask old men about hunting buffalo. There are many here who know about hunting buffalo."

Wow, there were people here who had hunted buffalo? I thought. Without thinking, I asked, "Which ones?" I wanted to know.

"I'm sure you will find them," said Iron Eyes Cody.

"Thank you, Sir," I said. My mind was now spinning as much as it was a few moments ago. Then all of a sudden, it occurred to me to ask him one more question. "What is the name of someone here who might tell me about buffalo hunting?"

Iron Eyes Cody seemed pleased that I had inquired further. "You should talk to Silver Horse." With that, he turned and walked away.

Us boys continued to walk around among the booths and artifacts. There were also demonstrations of dances and hunting techniques. Many dancers formed a large circle in colorful costumes. They wore large hoops of bright feathers, which added to the spectacle as they spun.

As the day of excitement came to a close, many spectators began to leave. The dancers were starting to take off their headdresses and ornate costumes. They began sitting in circles around the different fires that had been built. Near us was a cluster of people sitting down on their legs, preparing to eat. In the center of them was an older man. He was so wrinkled, I thought he could easily have been 100 years old. The clothes he wore were made of dried leather that was beginning to wither on the edges. More and more people were gathering around this man as if they were waiting to see what he might say. I joined the circle.

I never expected him to say anything to me. I wasn't even sure he could see. But all of a sudden, he turned to me and gestured, "welcome young man." I didn't say anything.

Was he talking to me? I wanted to be sure it was me he was addressing.

Then again, he turned to me and said, "I'm glad you're here. My name is Silver Horse."

"Silver horse? I have heard of you. I asked Iron Eyes Cody about buffalo hunting. He said he didn't know much about it, but if I get the chance, I should ask Silver Horse. It's a pleasure to meet you, Sir."

The old man smiled. "What is it you would like to know about buffalo hunting?"

I barely knew where to start. "Well, how you do it? Have you ever been?"

Silver Horse began to speak in his ancient voice. "Yes, I have been, but only a few times. The buffalo were mostly gone when I was a boy. I heard my grandfather's talk about them." Others in the circle were also fascinated by what he had to say. Quiet fell over them as he continued his story. The light of the fire near them illuminated their faces, but most especially the face of Silver Horse. His milky eyes were still but shining in the wavering light. He continued, "Hunting buffaloes here in the east was different than hunting with our brothers in the West. In the West, they would chase the herd and push them over cliffs. Then they got horses, and they were able to chase them even faster. Not in the east. There were not as many open spaces. In the east, we hunted the great buffaloes along the winding trails of our home. Yes, there were large herds, but those were hard to hunt. The ones that were hunted were in smaller herds."

"How did they hunt them?" One of the other listeners asked. Silver Horse straightened up his posture and took a deep breath.

"The most common way was for two hunters to hide on either side of the path. Another hunter would then begin to chase the buffalo down the path toward the hunters. The buffalo was made to be afraid. He would let down his guard for dangers in front of him due to his fear of what was behind him. When the buffalo came to the hunters, they would throw their spears at the same time."

Many of the people of the circle began to mumble to themselves. Each one picturing themselves in that position, and wondered if they would be able to spear a buffalo as it ran down a path past them.

"Is that what you wanted to know about hunting buffaloes?" asked Silver Horse.

"Yes Sir," I replied.

"Do you think you could hunt a Buffalo?" he asked.

"No, Sir, I don't think so. Seems dangerous. Did many hunters get hurt or killed hunting buffaloes like this?"

"Sometimes," replied Silver Horse, "but in those days, there was an agreement." No one was sure at first what he meant by this.

"What kind of agreement?" asked one of the others.

"Well, now that is a long story." Everyone wondered if Silver Horse would continue. The light of the day had now gone. It was dark. They were sure he was hungry, but his countenance revealed pleasure from the young listeners' questions. He then turned to me. "Would you like to hear it?" he asked.

"Yes, please!" I said. The crowd was silent. The nearby fire crackled as the beat of distant drumming and singing was heard in the distance. The old man took a few breaths and began to speak. These were his words:

In my time, the buffalo were almost gone. We knew about them from songs and stories. When we sang, our grandfathers told us about the buffalo. We wanted to know about our ancestors and how they hunted. To us, they seemed brave that they would hunt in this way. Our grandfathers told us of times in the past when buffalo were plentiful. Then he told of other times when buffalo were scarce. One particular time in the distant past, when there were not many buffaloes to be found, a member of our tribe met the Gray Buffalo. It is with the Gray Buffalo that our people had an agreement.

Many generations ago, a great chief was hunting buffalo with his two sons. They were hunting in the traditional way when they saw a young buffalo. The two sons hid on either side of the trail. Their father walked in a great circle through the woods, eventually coming to the trail on the other side of the buffalo. He then walked slowly and silently up the trail. When the young buffalo saw the Chief, it became afraid and ran away from him down the trail toward the sons. The buffalo was not looking for dangers ahead when it neared the spot where the sons lay waiting. It only feared the danger behind it. The buffalo was unaware of the two sons until they threw their spears. Their spears hit the mark, and within a few steps, the buffalo had fallen.

As the father came up the trail, he found the sons celebrating their kill. They were dancing and boasting that they were great buffalo hunters. They stood on top of the dying buffalo and waived their spears. They jumped up and down on the head of the beast, declaring they were more powerful than any animal. They skinned the creature with great haste and pride. They tossed the head and horns on one side of the trail, and the liver and entrails on the other. They kept only the hide and choice meat as they carried their prize toward their village, three days walk away.

That night the Chief and his two sons built a great fire. They roasted pieces of the meat and filled their bellies. They reveled and told stories of great hunters and declared they too were mighty hunters. When they became tired, they lay down next to their warm fire. With their stomachs full, they slept contently.

As the moon came higher into the night sky, their dreams were interrupted by a howling wind. When they awoke, they beheld a large gray buffalo standing right in front of them. His eyes were fixed upon the three of them and looked as if he was ready to charge. The chief and his two sons were terrified. Instead of killing them instantly with his horns, the creature spoke. "You killed my son!" The chief was unable to speak because he was trembling so, but eventually, he gathered the strength to mutter words.

"We are sorry! We are hunters. It is our way." said the Chief.

"You ate my son!" said the Gray Buffalo.

"Yes, we are men. We must eat to survive. It is our way." said the Chief.

"You danced when he died!" Screamed the Gray Buffalo. To this, the Chief had no answer, for he was ashamed they had danced upon the body of his son. The chief was working up his courage to speak more words to the Gray Buffalo when the oldest of his two sons reached for his spear.

"Because we are great!" Shouted the son as he stood and hurled his spear at the Gray Buffalo. The great beast dodged the spear and vanished into the dark night. The sons again celebrated their bravery and greatness.

The next morning when they were walking proudly down the trail carrying the meat, the Gray Buffalo suddenly appeared and was charging for them. Before they could grab their spears, the beast was upon them. With one swing of his great head, he tossed the Chief to one side of the trail. The beast then thrashed his head the other direction, giving a wallop to the oldest son tossing him off of the trail. The Chief and the oldest son lay motionless on the ground, unable to move as the Gray Buffalo charged toward the youngest son. He tossed the youngest son high into the air with his horns, and when the son hit the ground, the Gray Buffalo began to dance upon him.

The Chief and his remaining son could only watch. Their bodies were broken and bleeding from having been tossed by the buffalo. The Gray Buffalo continued dancing joyfully upon the body of the dead son. He danced and kept dancing. He danced and stomped until the body became trodden into the ground. The Gray Buffalo continued to dance until there was no remaining part of the son left in the muddy earth. Then the Gray Buffalo vanished.

The Chief and the son expressed deep sadness and were not able to travel very far due to their pain and grief. They decided to set up camp and build another fire only a short way down the trail and try to travel the next day. The Chief sat up late into the night, mourning the death of his son. When his pain and grief exhausted him, he found sleep. But this sleep was not to be! As soon as evening fell, they were wakened by the same howling wind, and there was the Gray Buffalo. Again, he spoke. "You killed my son!"

"Yes, and you killed mine!" shouted the Chief with all his might.

"You ate my son!" said the Gray Buffalo.

"Yes, it is our way! We are hunters! We will eat many more of your sons!" shouted the Chief.

"You danced when he died!" growled the Gray Buffalo.

"We were wrong, but you can harm us no more," said the Chief as his rage grew. The Chief reached for his spear and hurled it at the Gray Buffalo, but disappeared into the night.

The next day, the chief and his remaining son continued slowly toward their village. Both were very troubled by pain and grief. When, suddenly, just like the day before, the Gray Buffalo appeared.

The beast charged toward the Chief again, hitting him in the chest with his great horns tossing him from the trail. The brute then charged toward the oldest son and plunged his horns into his heart. The Buffalo tossed the son in the air and began to dance upon him when he came to the ground. He danced just as he had before. Again, the Chief was unable to do anything as the creature danced. Soon, nothing remained of his other son.

The Chief wailed. He could not move. His body was broken. He could not stand on his legs. He just lay there in the woods where the Buffalo had tossed him. He was unable to sleep because his pain and grief were so great, but when darkness fell, the Buffalo appeared again. "You killed my son."

"Yes, and you killed two of mine," spoke the Chief amid tears.

"You eat my sons!"

"Yes, it was our way, but you have killed us, and we will eat no more," moaned the Chief.

"You dance when they die!" spoke the Buffalo.

"We did not know of your greatness, but you have killed my sons and me," said the Chief accepting his death.

"I will kill many more of the sons of your tribe!" shouted the Gray Buffalo. The Chief was now even more grief-stricken. He knew the Gray Buffalo was powerful. The beast had killed his two sons, and the Chief knew the beast spoke the truth when he said he would kill many more.

"Why you evil Beast?" begged the Chief.

"Because you are prideful!" said the Gray Buffalo.

"What can I do to show you we are sorry. What can I do so you will not kill any more of the sons of my tribe?"

"You live. Go back to your village. Tell them what has happened here. Tell them how you danced when you killed my son. Then tell them how I danced when I killed your sons, and how I stomped them into the ground. You must tell your people of my greatness, and they must celebrate the death of your sons when I stomped them into the earth. The sons of your tribe must do this before hunting, or I will kill them just as I did your sons.

"I will tell them. We will remember what you have done." The Chief turned and put his face into the ground and wept. The Gray Buffalo vanished.

The Chief was unable to stand for two days, but on the third day, he was able to stand and begin his journey back to the village. When he arrived, the tribesman saw his injuries. They wept and cried aloud with great tears when they heard the sons had been killed. They were in disbelief when the Chief told how it happened and what the Gray Buffalo had told him. It terrified them. They knew the Chief was a great man and very brave. If the Gray Buffalo had done this to him, the creature could do it to them. They wanted no more harm to come to the sons of the tribe, so they all agreed to do what the Buffalo had told them.

The tribe made costumes out of buffalo hide and powdered it with the gray ash from the fire. The next time they needed meat and were going to hunt the buffalo, they did not forget their obligation. They placed buffalo horns on their head and put on the ashy gray buffalo skins. In these costumes, they danced around the fire as if they were the Gray Buffalo. They stomped the ground commemorating the trampling of the two sons into the earth. They continued this dance into the night until they were exhausted.

The next morning, they went on their hunt. Their hunt was successful, and none of the sons of their tribe were injured. Through the generations, they continued this ceremony and dance. They found as long as the tribe's hunters remembered the greatness of the Gray Buffalo and danced in celebration as he had commanded, they had a good hunt, and no one was hurt.

That was the arrangement.

Telling the story exhausted Silver Horse. After he spoke the final words, he sat quietly and watched the faces of those around him who were amazed by his parable. He looked at me but asked no more questions. I was too astonished to have any more questions for him. It was soon time to leave for home, but before doing so, I waved goodbye to Silver Horse, and he waved kindly back to me. I never saw him again, but I never forgot the story he told and the lesson it carried.

Chapter 10

Japanese Bullet

"Granddaddy?"

"Hmm?"

"How did you get that scar on your knee?" A weathered hand felt through the hole in his faded Levi jeans. He ran his index over a one-inch scar on his knee.

"This one?" he asked.

"Yes," I said. The faded pants were threadbare on both knees but the one I was looking at was on his right. I expected him to say something like, "I cut it on the fence" or "a saw fell on it," but he didn't. He was hesitant to tell me, and only stared at me for a moment.

"A Japanese bullet," he said. He was leaned back in his recliner whose white stuffing was coming out of the padded arms. He said nothing else and returned attention to the Louis Lamour paperback he held. He hoped the response he gave would preempt more questions from me.

A bullet, what in the world? I thought. I was sitting in Grandmother's chair, an equally ragged recliner, next to his, while she was adding onions to a crockpot. The room smelled of soup with lots of black pepper, mingled with the smoke of his Benson and Hedges cigarette. His answer of "a bullet" distracted me from the mid-day public television programming I was watching.

"How did you get it?" I continued.

He at first said nothing and was obviously reluctant to answer. "A Japanese Zero hit me in the knee."

"When?"

"When I was nineteen."

"What were you doing?"

"I was in a plane. Why do you want to know about that?" he gruffed.

"Was it when you were in the army?" Hoping this would give a clue.

"Air Corps," he said.

"Were you drafted?"

"No, I enlisted."

I certainly did not want to annoy him, and he obviously did not want to talk about it, but to an eleven-year-old boy this was too sensational to ignore. "Do you not like to talk about it?" I asked.

"I don't want Mother and Polly to hear about it." That was not the answer I expected. Polly was his wife of over forty years, and my grandmother.

"Why don't you want Granny and Grandmother to know about it?"

"It might upset them. What is it *you* want to know about it?" he asked, now annoyed.

"How you got it and what happened?" I asked sheepishly. He did not reply. "Were you a pilot?"

"No, a belly gunner. But that's not when we got shot down. I was a radio man in a C-47 flying over Burma when it happened."

"Why did you join the Air Corps?"

"Well, I didn't want to, but I didn't want to go to the regular Army and if I was drafted that is where I would go."

"Did everybody your age get drafted?"

"Not all at once, but you knew you would get the call eventually. In the Army you had to march, and I didn't care anything about that. So, I enlisted in the Army Air Corps, and had a little more choice about things."

"Did you want to fly planes?"

"No, I was hoping just to work on them, but they put me in for training as belly-gunner on the B-17. I flew around a few times, but I was too tall. I didn't fit in the glass bubble on the bottom the plane. I couldn't see because my knees were in the way. I'm not sure why they thought that was a good idea. I was too tall. I eventually put in for a transfer, and they sent me to radio school. My job was to send messages from plane to plane."

"What kind of messages?"

"In tap-code."

"Like S.O.S.?" I asked.

191

"Morse Code," he corrected.

"Do you still know it?"

"Not really, it's been too long."

"How did they train you?"

"Well, the code wasn't too hard, we just practiced with each other, and it came quick, but we had to know how to take the radios apart and replace the parts."

"Did they yell at you?" As a youngster my limited knowledge of the military came from television, and what made the biggest impression on me was that they yelled at trainees. To a kid, getting yelled at was far more intimidating than getting shot at.

"Not so much in radio school, they just complained. In basic they yelled though. A bunch. Those sergeants were some of the meanest and awfullest sort they had."

"What did they do?"

"Just yell at you about everything, try to find something you are doing wrong, and yell at you some more?"

"Did they ever yell at you?"

"I stayed out of trouble, but they yelled at all of us."

"You never got in trouble?"

"Not really. Well one time. I had to shave in front of a tree."

"What?" I was not sure what he meant.

"We had this old mean sergeant. We were all lining up for morning inspection when he came up to me and ask me if someone stole my razor. I didn't shave that morning and didn't think anyone would notice my few blond whiskers, but *he* did. He told me to go get my razor and come back. When I returned, he pointed over to a tree and said, 'pretend there is a mirror on that tree and shave your face.' So, I had to shave my face, dry, in front of that tree. It was a bloody mess when I was done."

"Did they ever beat you up?"

"No, I was taller than most of them, and I was pretty stout." He laughed and said, "We had another old sergeant who taught us boxing. He lined us up in pairs, but I knocked them all down. He came up to me and asked if 'I thought I was a tough guy.' I said, 'no.' He was a sparring partner for Sonny Liston, or so he said, and he had the flattened nose to back it up. He wasn't scared of anybody, and came up and got in my face, and asked again if I was tough. He just stood there and said nothing. I thought I would be smart, so I punched him right in the nose, and he fell flat on his back. We were both surprised for a second, then he jumped up and knocked me dizzy." This tale brought him a laugh, and he hoped it would satisfy my curiosity, and the subject could be changed.

"When did you get shot down?" I persisted. He paused and stared at his young interviewer.

"After I transferred. And I wasn't supposed to be in that plane." He no longer stared at his book but looked toward the kitchen to see who else was in hearing distance. Just above a whisper he continued, "I had a friend that drank a bunch of beer the night before he was supposed to take his turn operating the radio. It was for a flight across the mountains, and he felt mighty rough the next day. So, he asked if I would take his place. I had been up a few times, so I told him I would. We were flying what they called 'The Hump[12].' The C-47 was a cargo plane, and we were based in somewhere in India not far from the Burmese border. Whatever we were carrying had to go from our base to an airfield somewhere in China, then we would fly back."

"Where is Burma?" I asked.

"Tucked down in the corner somewhere between India and China."

"Did your airplane have machine guns?"

"Nope, we were hauling blankets and medicine, that's why the plane had the red cross painted on the side, but the Zeros didn't care about that. They would shoot down anything."

"Why are they called Zeros?"

"The Jap planes had a big red circle painted on the side, it was the same as their flag, and it looked like a big Zero."

"What happened when the Zeros shot at your plane?"

---

[12] "Flying the Hump" was an airlift effort during WWII to supply allied troops based in China with equipment from India. The massive effort was necessary after Japan destroyed the Burma Road. Cargo planes were frequently harassed by attacks from Japanese aircraft. The "Hump" was so named because the flightpath crossed the Himalayan Mountains. Even without the threat of Japanese air attacks, the flight was perilous due to the severe Himalayan weather as well the lack of sufficient radio navigation aids.

"Well, as we were flying along, the navigator was looking out of the window and noticed two Zeros. He went up and told the two pilots. I guess they tried to get away from them, but it seemed like only a few seconds later that the Zeros started shooting. You could hear the machine guns, even though there were no bullets hitting us at first. Then all of a sudden, we felt the plane jerk as they shot up one of the engines. Then another Zero came at an angle from the left side and shot at the cockpit from real close. They shot out the glass and killed the pilots, so we knew we had to bail out."

"With a parachute?"

"Yes."

"Had you ever used a parachute before that?"

"Nope."

"Were you scared?"

"Of course! It was the worst feeling I'd ever had in my life, before or since. I still have nightmares about it."

"Where were you when you had to jump?"

"I'm still not completely sure, it was somewhere over north Burma. I *did* know that wherever I was jumping into would be swarming with Japs, so I didn't like the idea very much."

"Were you the first to jump out?"

"No. The navigator had his chute on first and bailed out pretty fast. But the Zero that shot up the cockpit got him. When he jumped, he pulled the chord immediately, but the Zero swung around and shot him in the air after his chute opened. As I was watching all of this happening, the Jap that shot the engine was still shooting, and a bullet ricocheted off of the shell of the plane and laid my knee open. It knocked me back inside the plane, so I had to get up again to jump. I knew the Zeros would get me, just like they did the other fella, when I pulled my chute. So, when I jumped, I grabbed the chord, but kept telling myself 'wait, wait, wait.'"

His voice was shaking, as he described pulling the chord. His right hand was balled into a fist as if holding the pull-chord of the parachute and as he recounted "wait, wait, wait." His arm and white-knuckled fist flinched slightly with each word.

"I don't even remember floating down on the parachute, it was so quick. I had waited until the last possible moment to pull the chord, and had made it past the Zeros, but I hit the ground really hard. I was alive, but man oh man, my knee hurt. It was bleeding like crazy and it hurt to move it."

"What about the other guy, that jumped out before you?" I asked.

"My first thought was to try to find him. I saw where he landed because he hit the ground after me. I could hardly walk because of the knee, so I had to hop, but I made my way toward him. I found him, but he was shot up badly, and making a bunch of racket. I knew this would attract the Japs. I tried to get him to be quiet, but he was out of it from blood loss. As best I could, I dragged him into some bushes, trying to hide him from the Japs on the ground that saw our parachutes, and were sending a patrol to find us. Because he was being so loud, I knew I had to get away from him and find my own place to hide. Well, sure enough, here they came. They heard the other fella moaning and found him. Then they spread out and started looking for me."

"Did they take the other fella prisoner?"

"No, they bayonetted him."

"Did you run?"

"No, I couldn't my knee hurt too badly. I found a little creek, and started limping downstream as best I could, until I found a good hiding spot. I eventually found one; there was a flat rock jutting out of the bank of the stream, just above the water line, and it had a little space under it - so I wedged myself in there. I guess it worked because they didn't find me. I could hear them barking orders at each other when they walked by, and I could even see their boots."

"How long did you stay there?"

"A few hours, I knew I had to wait until dark before I started moving. After the Japs moved on, I crawled out from under the rock and got a look at my knee. I still remember it. The skin was peeled back and the bullet made a grove in the kneecap. The bleeding was slowing down but it hurt more and more, and it was swelling."

"Did you have a gun with you?"

"No."

"Did you have a backpack?"

"Nope, nothing."

"Did the Japs come back?"

"No, I never saw them again. After it got dark, I started hobbling down the stream. I was not even sure which way to go. I knew there were not any good guys around, so I figured it didn't matter. After a while, I saw a foot path that crossed the stream. Instead of boot prints, it had tracks of bare feet in the mud. So, I thought I would follow the trail for a bit."

"Where did the trail lead?"

"I never found out. I imagine it just went on for miles, perhaps to a village or something, but I don't know."

"Did anyone see you?"

"Yes eventually. I was still moving slow because of my knee, but I would go a little way, and then freeze and listen. If anyone was coming, I wanted to hear them first. I never heard anything. I was getting exhausted, and the trail just went on and on, so when I saw a little hedge of trees that looked like I could climb into them, I did. It was off of the trail a little way and was thick enough that you couldn't see in through the limbs. I climbed up into it and rested there and listened. I never heard anything, so I eventually went to sleep. Right at sunup, I was awakened by four men gathering around the tree where I was. I assumed the Japs had found me because they looked at me with squinty eyes. But they had no shoes, didn't wear uniforms, and looked about as hungry as I was. I still remember them all smiling as they looked up at me in the tree. One of them gestured for me to come down. I assumed now that they weren't Japs, or they would have just shot me. They helped me out of the tree and notice my knee. One of them poured a packet of sulfa powder under the fold of skin. Then another gave me a drink of water out of a G.I. canteen – but I later saw him fill up the canteen in the creek, he had just given me creek water. Whatever, creepy-crawlies were in that water I drank, gave me diarrhea for the next thirty years."

"They were on our side?"

"Yes, it turns out they were part of the Burmese Underground. They helped me hobble along for a few days until they got me help. I don't remember all the journey after that, but I remember a few days later I was in a jeep on the way to a tent hospital; and then on a plane; and then in another hospital. After a couple of weeks, I could walk, and then it wasn't long until they shipped me home."

"What did your family say when you told them about it?"

"Why, I never told them much about it. In fact, I've just told you more than I've ever told anyone. And you should just keep it to yourself."

"You never told Grandmother?"

"No."

"What did you do after you got home?"

"Well, I enrolled in Harding College in Arkansas. I met your grandmother while I was there."

"Why did you choose Harding College?"

"It was a college for preachers, and when I was in that tree in Burma, I made a deal with the Lord."

"What kind of deal?"

Tears filled his eyes. "I prayed and said, 'Lord if you get me out of this I will work in your service.'"

After that I was silent. I had heard the most fascinating thing I had ever heard. He also was silent as he stared at the wall, thinking. I am sure he was thinking of all the events in his life that were shaped by this experience. The nightmares, the hardships of being a poor preacher for many years just to fulfill a prayerful promise, all the places the job of preaching took him and his family. His stomach had ached continually for years due to an amoeba he contracted from the water the rescuers gave him. He coughed constantly with emphysema from the cigarettes he smoked one-after-the-other to calm his nerves. All this, from an experience of war as a nineteen-year-old.

"Daddy, supper's ready," said Grandmother from the kitchen.

"Well, let's go eat," he said. "Let's not tell anyone about what we talked about."

Chapter 11

Sensible Stranger

*D*ew covered the green fields of Cambridge, Massachusetts on the morning of June 16th, 1780. The warm smell of a summer morning greeted a new future for everyone in the state. The day before, the voters of Massachusetts had approved the new state's constitution. They had rejected the previously submitted version, and returned its writers to the drawing board. Now they had accepted the latest, historically unprecedented, list of statutes that would rule their lives into the future. The journey to complete the document had been long and arduous, but in the coming years it would be an inspiration and model for the Constitution of the United States. Thirty gentlemen from the state's towns were selected to create the Constitution of the Commonwealth of Massachusetts, and the result was a set of rules that provided for the greater good by separating powers in legislative, judicial, and executive branches. This template would become the nidus of genius used to create the greatest democratic civilization the world has ever known, when the United States adopted the template for its Constitution.

The ancestors of these thirty creators were the puritans, who averse to tyranny, sojourned to the New World. Now, they were currently enthralled in a bloody war for independence from England, and there was much uncertainty whether or not they would prevail. They had become familiar with war, yet they yearned for a prosperous peace. War was not their only worry. There were many hurdles that made the completion of the state constitution difficult. Factions existed among them that had to be reconciled, spirits of violence had to be tamed, and fears of creating a government that could eventually oppress them had to be appeased. Many times, when they were gathered, the task seemed futile as agreement could not be found. Nevertheless, they persisted in their endeavor to find the words that defined their wishes for the future. Little did they know, two centuries later, the offspring of this effort would be studied and revered as a gem for the ages.

Collected personal letters and diaries of the authors recount the many hardships and brutal arguments that fomented before the final terms coalesced onto parchment. These private words reveal the many thoughts and opinions shared, and debated, among the delegation. Some of the men wrote their thoughts, while others only exchanged their contemplations among secret circles. In both the written accounts and oral traditions, they frequently allude to a speaker who came to them with words and ideas that propelled them toward common unity. His name was never given, nor was his nation of origin, but he came from the Old World with a message for them. In October of 1779, this unknown voice of reason appeared when encouragement was needed to lift them from dissuasion, and amalgamate their convictions into a final declaration. One of the thirty wrote:

"After nearly a month, it appeared we were no closer to a resolution than on the day we began our debates. Would the body politic reject our deliberations, we knew not. Discouragements abounded and many clamored that a solution would not be found before we were all hanged for treason. The day of the arrival of the foreign visitor began with a morning that abused us wrathfully with dilemma, but his words were so laden with truth, and sweet to the ears, that thereafter a spirit united us and sped our efforts toward fruition."

Those that knew who he was never said it aloud or wrote it down. No record of who invited him to speak was ever made, however, it is apparent that all of them were in awe of his words. Some have said he was from the academe of

Edinburgh[13], or possibly a Martinist[14] from France, while others claimed him to be a high-ranking member of a European Masonic order. Perhaps it was the mysterious Comte de St. Germain[15], who supposedly made a visit with similar effect in Philadelphia to the Continental Congress. Whomever he was, he had come from afar, and when he arrived, he was greeted warmly and thanked for his arduous journey aboard ship. His dress was of a foreign ilk, and his speech bore a mixture of accents. As he entered the room where they were gathered, he was greeted warmly as a brother. They thanked him vehemently for his coming despite the risks; they knew traveling by ship was treacherous and imprisonment was threatening as the Atlantic coast of New England was thick with ships of the British Navy. No formal introduction of him was made to the group, and his name was not used. Some among the number did not know who he was nor who invited him, but those that did gushed with awe. His demeanor was benevolent as he addressed the group.

---

[13] The University of Edinburgh, Scotland was a center for the study of economics, capitalism, and nation building during the mid to late 1700's. The scene's most famous contributor was Adam Smith. He is considered a philosopher who during the Scottish Enlightenment wrote *The Theory of Moral Sentiments* and *[The] Wealth of Nations*. These works are considered the foundation stone of capitalist democracy.

[14] Martinism was an esoteric Christian movement that grew rapidly in France and Russia during the mid to late 1700's. Veiled in Masonic secrecy, it concerned the improvement of mankind by encouraging thought and contemplation and other cryptic philosophies.

[15] The Comte de St. Germain was a title used by more than one person during the revolutionary period of the 1700's. The name is associated with leaders of the European Freemasons, Knight Templar, and Rosicrucian orders.

Some of the words he spoke have been pieced together from the many sources that contain fragments. Though surely not all of his words are recorded, those that were recollected were thus:

"Brothers, I thank you on behalf of myself, and the countless souls who do not yet know your labors. We across the sea are mindful of your current fight against tyranny, and may it please you to know, our hearts are united with yours. May it also please you to know, the King's[16] resolve is weak, and there is much grumbling from his ministers that to persist in the retention of these colonies is futile. Even now, the *Roi de France at de Navarre*[17] loads his ships for your aide. Rest assured, brothers, the end of this conflagration is in sight. Brute facts cannot refute your resolve. Moreover brothers, when the day of battle is over, we must transcend our base desires and return to the plow. We must become *Cincinnatus*[18], for you cannot be a hostile people and survive. Your continent will soon enjoy peace, yet the fire of war will return across the sea. I say to you, we cannot control our neighbors but we can control ourselves. Do not join the fray, but let shine the destiny within you. Let

---

[16] This obviously refers to King George III of England.
[17] Louis XVI, the King of France.
[18] Refers to Lucius Quinctius Cincinnatus who left his beloved farm to serve as a successful Roman general, then after peace was obtained, he gladly returned to his plow.

tyrants consume themselves with the cannon, while you sow the seeds of peace. Never before has the weight of mankind's future rested upon the shoulder of so few. The survivors of kingdoms laid waste will look to your example, and will emulate the laws of peaceful existence you are tasked to compose. Mind your words, for they dictate whether there is peace or war; whether your children prosper or suffer conflict; and whether your people rise like Atlantis or live in ignorance. There are likely conflicts between you, and arise from scars suffered in the past, and cut so deeply the future cannot heal them, but let reason remove the distance between your actions and your morals. Remove that which separates what you say from what you know in the depth of your soul. History has shown that empires rise and inevitably must fall. In due course all Tyrants have succumbed to the wrath of the trodden. Brothers, the time of your empire is now. Never before has such a land as yours appeared with such inherent wealth and spirit. Citizens, you will lead the minds of lovers of peace for eons or you will replicate the follies of the unwise. The conscience of the world is ripe to receive direction. Give much charity to the advice of the men that join you in this room, for this is manger into which the future of peace and prosperity will be laid in its infancy."

The mysterious stranger apparently did not linger long in Cambridge, but his words had great effect. After his eloquent encouragements, the group of thirty soon produced the Constitution they were tasked with creating. In the remaining days of their deliberations, they agreed in increasing unanimity with how the future law of the land should be composed. The man who finally inked his goosequill to compose the lines was none other than future President John Adams. In the closing days of October 1779, while the Continental Army struggled against the British, and likely would have failed if it were not for the intervention of France, Adams wrote with a steady hand the opening words of the Constitution of the Commonwealth of Massachusetts. They began:

> The end of the institution, maintenance, and administration of government, is to secure the existence of the body politic, to protect it, and to furnish the individuals who compose it with the power of enjoying in safety and tranquility their natural rights, and the blessings of life: and whenever these great objects are not obtained, the people have a right to alter the government, and to take measures necessary for their safety, prosperity and happiness.
>
> The body politic is formed by a voluntary association of individuals: it is a social compact, by which the whole people covenants with each citizen, and each citizen with the whole people, that all shall be governed

by certain laws for the common good. It is the duty of the people, therefore, in framing a constitution of government, to provide for an equitable mode of making laws, as well as for an impartial interpretation, and a faithful execution of them; that every man may, at all times, find his security in them.

We, therefore, the people of Massachusetts, acknowledging, with grateful hearts, the goodness of the great Legislator of the universe, in affording us, in the course of His providence, an opportunity, deliberately and peaceably, without fraud, violence or surprise, of entering into an original, explicit, and solemn compact with each other; and of forming a new constitution of civil government, for ourselves and posterity; and devoutly imploring His direction in so interesting a design, do agree upon, ordain and establish the following *Declaration of Rights, and Frame of Government,* as the Constitution of the Commonwealth of Massachusetts.

These words were among the first rules governing a society of free citizens that separated the branches of government, and provided a guarantee for the practice of democratic capitalism. John Adams who penned these words, would be among the trio[19] who composed the same for the United States of America. Who knows how much the words of the mysterious stranger contributed to these documents, and if the secret brotherhood to which he may have belonged,

---

[19] The trio consisted of John Adams, Benjamin Franklin, and Thomas Jefferson.

facilitated the knowledge that led to the success of the Constitutions, but without doubt, those who were there, remember the effect the words of the sensible stranger had on their hearts and minds.

Chapter 12

Big Claude

From a nursing home bed, an eighty-nine year old Ruth Calhoun was talkative. Her faculties were dimmed by age, yet with tearful details she recounted the story of her son Claude. Claudius Alton Calhoun was born in 1882. They were a poor farming family in rural Iowa, and he would be their only son. The family's farm was a few miles east of Wallingford and bordered Lake Ingham. As an infant and toddler, young Claude was quite normal, and his early boyhood was typical of those growing up on a remote farm on the plains; there were neighbors a half-mile away in any direction, but none had children Claude's age, so, when he played, it was mostly by himself. However, it did not seem to bother Claude, as his favorite pastime was to swim in the lake, enjoying his own company.

His parents, John and Ruth Calhoun, spent their life raising hogs. Many of their neighbors grew corn or wheat, but John and Ruth lacked sons, and therefore lacked the strong arms and abilities a big family could offer. With little money to hire additional hands, raising pigs suited them as they were better able to manage the work themselves. They found it more profitable to sell the pigs on foot as opposed to selling them as hams or sausage. Therefore, there were lots of pigs, and as a result, the typical odor of a pig farm permeated the air around them. However, Claude did not mind; he knew no different. He found contentment watching the small animals that played in the dusk light at the edge of the neighbor's cornfield.

When Claude was eleven, he began getting headaches. They were only occasional at first, and his parents did not think much of it. "You're having a growth spurt. It's just growing pains that you're feeling," his parent suggested. However, when his headaches intensified and became more frequent, John and Ruth became concerned, and even more so when they noticed the pitch of his voice lowering and the growth of hair under his arms. Although still so young, he appeared very fit and muscular, and noticeably taller than anyone his age. Over the next year, his rapid height growth continued, and by the time he was thirteen, he was as tall as his father and was growing facial hair. They took him to a local doctor, but he could find no explanation, and in those days, options for treatment were nonexistent.

By age fifteen, he was seven feet tall and had a low gravelly voice. His facial features began to coarsen, and the hair on his head thinned. In another year, he was eight feet tall. By now, the aches of his unusually large body plagued him constantly and affected his agility. He begged to do his school lessons at home after becoming terribly self-conscious of his size and baldness. When the family went into Wallingford, he cried not to go and be subjected to gasps and jeers.

In those days, circuses and freak shows searched for individuals with unique abnormal physical appearances. Claude knew of them and developed great anxieties about being pestered by them. His parents agreed that his extreme height would draw the attention of gawkers. At sixteen years, he was ten feet tall and still muscular, but his face had become quite grotesque. The skin of his forehead, cheeks, and shoulders was pocked with large pustules of acne. Claude grew increasingly fearful of being seen, and his parents obliged his request to remain hidden. When he was nineteen, he was fourteen feet tall. Clothing him became difficult, and he stayed ravenously hungry. He no longer fit in his bed, and to sit at the kitchen table was impossible. He found it more comfortable to sleep in the barn, with its high ceilings accommodating his height, and there was room for him to stretch out when sleeping. His headaches were now constant, and his bones hurt continually.

Claude wanted nothing more than to hide from the outside world as his fear of being seen intensified. His parents also thought this was best. Soon, he would only come out of the barn at night, afraid that if he was outside during the day, a neighbor passing by the dirt road in front of their house might see him. Through all the ups and downs, John and Ruth remained simple folks who loved their son and wanted to protect him, understanding his fears and his pleas to conceal himself. They had their own unease of potential public taunting if it were known what Claud had become. Since they feared the unwanted attention the family would get if their son was seen, they supported his desire to only come out at night.

After their agreement, Claude's spirits lifted a bit, and he was more helpful around the farm, doing chores in the moonlight. Though his muscles and bones ached, his size rendered him strong compared to a regular-sized man. He fashioned a board to a forked branch and could make quick work of pushing the loose muck out of the hog pen – a chore that would have taken John much longer. Claude could also make repairs on the roof without the risk of a fall since he required no ladder, which proved helpful after many Iowa storms.

At age seventeen, he began having seizures. His episodes began as collapsing and shaking violently every few days, but the episodes became more frequent and became a daily fright for his parents. While helping his father tend to the pigs in the dark, it was not unusual to have two or three thrashing fits during his waking hours. In a plea for help, his parents wrote a letter to the doctor informing him of Claude's unusual height growth and his seizures. The doctor replied that he likely had a tumor causing the symptoms, and contrary to their hopes, there was nothing to do about it. At twenty-one years old, he was sixteen feet tall. Each year he grew.

His parents did what they could to improve his comfort, and although they yearned for him to be in the safety and warmth of their house, he simply did not fit. Doing what she could to improve his sorrowful existence, Ruth sewed quilts together to make him a sleep cover big enough to fit him. To separate him from the pigs and grime, John and Claude constructed a false wall in the back of the barn. In his hidden room, if an unlikely visitor were to look into the barn, they would not notice a living quarter in the rear. This pleased Claude and allowed him a private and quiet place, separate from a world that would mock him.

His vision had become so poor that reading was difficult. Even holding books was awkward due to the size of his hands. Instead, his condition condemned him to sit in quiet contemplation. Many men his age dreamed of girls or traveling to far-off places, but Claude dreamed of the opposite. He wanted never to be seen.

The tumor in Claude's head secreted growth hormones at a much higher rate than normal. The effects made him very large, and deformed in many ways. His hands were unnaturally massive with long thin fingers that grew to over a foot long each. His disproportionately long arms were gangly and crooked, and his legs were spindly and bowed. His head had become completely bald except for coarse sideburns that grew in thick mats upon his jowls. The skin of his face and scalp thickened and formed redundant folds and wrinkled ravines of flesh that flaked and stank. Painful pustules ruptured and oozed, leaving odorous sores that scarred. Large flaking patches of crusty skin formed around his nose and in the folds of his neck that burned with relentless irritation. The skin of his body was much the same, and the sweat and grime from his chores tending swine aggravated his many festering lesions. The largeness of his genitals, with their pestering thrush, stung as they were knocked about by his bowed legs. The toenails growing from his enormous feet and toes were as thick as bars of soap, making them almost impossible to cut and they too stayed constantly infected. His putrid smell was intense and often overpowered the odor of the hogs.

His mother made clothes for him out of bed sheets and table cloths. She discovered the most practical way to cover him was to sew the sheets into a tunic. She made a sleeved cape out of quilts to keep him warm in the winter. Feeding him was no small endeavor either. He was always hungry. He grew skinny from the lack of calories available to him compared to that which his bulk needed. Ruth baked him two large loaves a day in addition to the continual cooking of stews. His father would roast whole pigs at a time on a spit. One roasted hog could supply Claude's ever-hungry body with protein for two or three days. The bony scraps of the carcasses were thrown back to the pigs, which they devoured completely.

One constant that proved to be a continual source of peace for Claude was to swim in the lake. The shore was about one hundred and fifty yards from the back of the barn. Occasionally during the day, a canoe or a rowboat could be seen with a lazy occupant fishing, but when night came, the lake belonged solely to Claude. His problems did not matter as much at night. Claude was able to let down his guard against being seen with the protection of darkness. The scrubby pasture between the barn and the lake was where he preferred to walk unseen. His tattered clothes, which barely covered him, were unnecessary after sundown.

The cold lake water on Claude's body temporarily soothed the itching and burning of his grotesque skin. Being too large for a tub, the lake provided a bathing solution during the summer months. Claude would sigh with relief as his buoyancy in the water relieved his joints from his great weight. His legs still touched the muddy bottom even several yards into the lake. In the summer, he went nightly, but in the winter the frosty nights prohibited him from going out and he longed for the warmer days when he could resume his daily swim. He often thought of trying to swim across to the other side but was afraid the exertion would bring on a seizure. A few times, he felt the prodrome of his seizures appear while in the water, and climbed out of the water and sat upon the bank, just in time for the overpowering fit to manifest.

Once, after coming out of a seizure, he sat upon the bank watching fish jump through the water, and ducks dip into its cool waves. He longed to share their home; his only wish was to stay in the comfort of the water, the only place he felt safe, unnoticed, and unobserved. In this peaceful tranquility, an idea formed. The lake would be a great place to disappear. To die. Die? No. He couldn't do that to his parents. But what if he just gave the appearance of it, only to the public? His parents would no longer have to deal with the public's watchful eye, those who wondered, "what has happened to Claude? I haven't seen him in so long." And for himself, he would no longer have to live in fear of being seen, of being harassed.

One evening while Claude was helping John sort hogs. His long arms and stork-like legs moved along, opening gates for the hogs when his slow, guttural voice began. "Father, you know how much I fear that someone will see me? If they do, they won't leave us alone."

"Yes, Son." There was a pause as John wondered why the question. He noticed Claude seemed more bothered about the topic than usual. "If they did see you, we would never let anyone bother you."

"Yes, but they would bother *you* with questions about me. They would think I was a monster." John said nothing, knowing this was true. Claude took a deep breath and stood tensely as he prepared himself for his father's response to his idea. "Father, I could drown in the lake," he began. "Not really, but what if we faked my death? I could drown only in ruse."

John's eyes bulged at the shock of his son's suggestion. "Claude! Why are you talking this ..." John did not finish his thought as the meaning of his son's words suddenly became clear. He pondered it. His silence indicated to Claude that he was weighing the possibility, so he dared to continue.

"I don't think it would be difficult." Claude continued his planned narrative. "We could say I was swimming in the lake. You warned me not to attempt to cross to the other side, but decided to go anyway. In the exhaustion of getting across, I felt a fit coming on, but I couldn't get back to the bank quickly enough."

"They would search. The sheriff would come," said John. Claude walked away from the hog lot to where he could see the lake. He pointed to a cove that was a distance from the house to the south.

"You watched me struggle, and I drifted to the south curve before I went under. You could tell people you saw me go under," explained Claude.

"It is a sin to lie, Son."

"It's a sin to be hunted, father." Irritated, Claude went back to the barn and nothing more was said of it that night. Claude could see the subject was killing John to discuss, and although it pained him to see his father chew over the thought of faking his own son's death, he knew it pained him more to witness the misery Claude felt every day. When John returned to the house, he related Claude's idea to Ruth. She was immediately against it.

"John, we can't just make up some story and lie to the law," she said.

"I know, and I agree, but it will make it easier for Claude," said John. The thought of her own son's death made her feel sick to her stomach. Yet, it pained her to admit, it would bring great relief to Claude if he was dead in the minds of the neighbors who knew of him. This way, no one would ask about him. With a great feeling of defeat, accompanied with a sigh, she admitted the lie would lessen some of her son's angst. She wondered what she could have done differently to lessen her son's pain. Was the world punishing her for something? She had tried to lead an honest life; she had abided by the laws of her community, volunteered for those in need, worked with those even less fortunate than her, yet the question of 'why?' plagued her almost every minute of every day. She just wanted what was best for her son.

Claude and John continued to discuss it in the nights to come, and after a month of painful yet careful deliberation, the family agreed it was for the best. In a brave effort, John drove his team of mules into town and reported the drowning to the sheriff, weeping genuine tears. The sheriff responded with sincere sympathy. "I'm sorry this has happened to you, John. You and Ruth are good people. I had heard that little Claude was having some spells. I guess he wasn't little though. How is Ruth taking it?"

"Well, for now, she is beside herself, but she is strong. She will be okay," John replied.

The sheriff kindly asked if they needed help looking for the body. John declined, saying they would handle any future discovery of the body and would keep the sheriff updated if it was found. He gave John a signed note he was to take to the courthouse to receive a death certificate. Now, as far as anyone knew, Claude was dead. A wave of relief washed over Claude, and for the first time in what felt like a lifetime, the corners of his lips turned upward. It had been years since he'd felt even the slightest hint of freedom. The abnormally tall son of the hog farmer was gone. They wondered how tall he was, imagining eight or ten feet, but it was only John and Ruth who knew he was over twenty-four feet tall. His room behind the false wall of the barn was now his only domain, but that was what Claude wanted.

At age twenty-seven, his growth continued, and his height was past twenty-eight feet tall. His severe body aches worsened to the point that he could barely rise out of bed. Sometimes he simply could not get up and would lay in filth for days. John and Ruth knew he could not live much longer like this. They dreaded the day when he could bear life no longer. They knew Claude's end of days was approaching but could not bear to speak of it. They each privately pondered the inevitable; how to deal with his body. How would they ever manage to dig a hole big enough?

Over the next two years, he became completely immobilized by pain and stiffness from the unyielding growth. His teeth rotted away, making it impossible to eat, or even come close to consuming the number of calories he needed. His large body grew thinner and more painful by the day. John scraped away the daily excrement in the same way Claude had done in the hog pen when he could still do chores.

John or Ruth was always by his side during his final days. His breathing was loud, and he painfully coughed up large mucous wads. John was by his side when he took his last breath. Tears streamed down his face as his only son left the world behind him, one that had treated him so cruelly. John knew the loss of Claude wasn't the only reason his tears fell; they fell for the suffering, the loneliness he was condemned to, and the physical pain that enslaved him for every second of his life. As his body grew still and cold, John left his son's side and went back into the house. Lying down next to Ruth, he did not have to say anything nor could he find the words. She knew Claude had passed. She felt a cold, deep hole grow in her heart, replacing the sense of warmth and comfort that only love and family had once brought her. Tears ran down her cheeks, a never-ending waterfall of emotion. Together, they lay still and silent. Hand in hand, they grieved the loss of their only son. In their silence, they remembered him as a baby. He was a playful little boy with the same hopes and dreams as any child. They also shared the gnawing thought of what to do with his body.

A night of silence passed between the couple; a silence which dragged into the morning. Neither could find a word to say, a topic to speak of, a happy thought to share. The death of their son hung over them, leaving them both in a fog of mindless existence.

Ruth was up first and made John breakfast. Finally, she spoke. "What are you planning to do?"

"I don't know yet."

"It will take all you've got to dig a hole big enough."

"It will take a few days," he said, staring dead ahead with little life left in his eyes.

"How will you move him?"

"I don't know that either."

She saw little point in wasting her breath on unanswered questions, so she held her tongue, watching John sip his morning coffee. After a few minutes of quiet contemplation, he rose slowly and walked outside. The morning was crisp, and John held onto his coffee tightly, grateful for the warmth of the cup heating his cold hands. Taking another sip, he leaned against the rail of the hog pen and watched as the pigs became livelier in his presence. 'I don't have scraps for you,' he said to them. They continued their wallowing and grunted complaints of hunger. While watching the pigs, an idea formed in his mind, but it was too vile to entertain. *What an insult to such a kind soul. He deserves better than that.* He tried to banish these thoughts, but the grim idea persisted as he stepped away from the pen and walked into the room of the barn where Claude's body lie.

He wept openly as he stood next to Claude, knowing he had no other option. "I'm sorry Son, you deserve better," he said. Tears rolled down his face as he grabbed a mallet. He began tearing down the wall that separated Claude's room from the rest of the barn. Once the wall was reduced to planks, he opened the hog gate and let the hungry pigs into the barn. He did not look back as he returned to the house.

Once inside, he sat down at the table. He had no appetite for breakfast. Ruth placed a hand on his shoulder.

"Any ideas?" she asked.

He did not answer until he gathered enough composure to speak. "I tore down the wall and let the pigs in."

Ruth looked at him in horror, yet she knew there were no other options.

Forty years later, the story of Claude might never have been known were it not for his mother, Ruth. She lived to be eighty-nine years old and spent her last days in a nursing home. In her final days, her mind was clouded by dementia, but she still enjoyed the company of the nurses that tended to her. For fifty years, she kept her son's story a secret. Her husband John had been dead twenty years. Perhaps it was dementia or the permission granted by a half-century of time, but she began talking about Claude. A nurse named Juanice was her favorite. Ruth told her about their farm in Iowa, as well as stories about John and Claude. Juanice initially dismissed the idea of Ruth having a son who was nearly thirty feet tall, for she knew Ruth was senile. However, her story was persistent. She told Juanice about his normal childhood. She described his headaches and seizures and that they suspected he had a tumor. Ruth recounted to her how Claude grew and grew. How he had to live in the barn and hide from the prying eyes of those who might tease him. She wept when she recounted how they had to fake his death. She had terrible pain in her eyes when she related how lonely he must've been. She laughed at the memory of the happy times and how he could patch the roof without a ladder. She sobbed when she described the pigs eating his body when he died. Her story was so vivid and consistent, Juanice could not help to think there might be an element of truth to it. Ruth never told the story of Claude to anyone else. Those memories, if they were real, died with her. Was it a figment of her senescence? Until her last day, she insisted it was true and could relate every detail consistently. It was so long ago, and at Ruth's age, who could be sure? Maybe it was true. Maybe it wasn't.

The End